The Lies I Never Told You

About the Author

Valérie Tong Cuong lives in Paris with her husband and four children. Her novels have garnered a number of literary awards and have been translated into eighteen languages. *The Lies I Never Told You* is her twelfth novel.

VALÉRIE TONG CUONG

The Lies I Never Told You

Translated from the French
by Maren Baudet-Lackner

HODDER

First published in the French language as *Les guerres
intérieures* by Jean-Claude Lattès in 2019

First published in Great Britain in 2020 by Hodder & Stoughton
An Hachette UK company

1

A CIP catalogue record for this title is available from the British Library

Paperback ISBN 9781529373288
eBook ISBN 9781529373295

Typeset in Plantin Light by Hewer Text UK Ltd, Edinburgh
Printed and bound in Great Britain by Clays Ltd, Elcograf S.p.A.

Hodder & Stoughton policy is to use papers that are natural, renewable
and recyclable products and made from wood grown in sustainable
forests. The logging and manufacturing processes are expected to
conform to the environmental regulations of the country of origin.

Hodder & Stoughton Ltd
Carmelite House
50 Victoria Embankment
London EC4Y 0DZ

www.hodder.co.uk

To Éric

My life is yours and yours is mine; you live what I live.
There is but one destiny.
So, take this mirror and study your reflection.

Victor Hugo (Preface to *Contemplations*, 1856)

A scream, yes

He hasn't experienced excitement like this in quite some time. It's a belligerent energy that sweeps aside his regrets, an intoxicating feeling that his lucky day has finally come to free him from a life of frustration. He's waited for so long, enduring humiliating rejections at auditions and snide comments on his lack of charisma, his high-pitched voice, and B-list CV. No one seemed to care that he'd been a part of a major TV series that caused the network's audiences to skyrocket. He's spent the past few decades alternating between silent rage and bitter nights huddled in the foetal position, or occasionally enjoying the fleeting pleasures of the flesh in the beds of women who are never those he dreamed of, but those whose dreams he fulfils.

When did he give up? He can't say exactly. He slid slowly but surely down a destructive slope from which there was no escape, the way the tree trunks and the bougainvillaea vines of the tropics bend helplessly to the will of the relentless wind.

But Pax will remember the exact moment when everything changed and a new path opened forever. On his deathbed, he will still have crystal-clear memories of 23 September 2017, when much to his colleague Elizabeth's dismay, his phone rang at work, interrupting an intense brainstorming session. He'll recall how hard he worked to control the inner turmoil the call provoked and the words he chose to cajole Elizabeth: *Sveberg wants to see me. I guess there really is a God!*

He laughed as if it were just a joke, but deep down he was certain it was a miracle.

Elizabeth closed her folders as her annoyance gave way to admiration and then satisfaction. She always thought she had made the right choice hiring him for Thea & Co. If he got this role, she would rewrite her pitch for the "Coaching Through Theatre" module. It would make an immediate impression on her clients, who would get a buzz from starring opposite an actor hired by Peter Sveberg. If he didn't get it, she would still play up the connection—getting noticed by a director with multiple Oscars was an accomplishment, no matter the outcome.

"Go," she said to Pax with a paternalistic smile, as if she were doing him a favour.

Elizabeth is a savvy businesswoman with dual qualifications as a psychologist and a life coach. She realized before anyone else what an important role theatre could play in companies, particularly given the rise of psycho-social risk in the workplace. One of the reasons for her success is her ability to detect people's vulnerabilities; the other is her knack for transforming and rewriting situations from different points of view. She was able to convince Pax to give up a Saturday afternoon to help her slog through her backlog, but he's the one who feels a little guilty as he rushes out of the office.

For the rest of his life, whenever he thinks about what happened next, he'll remember this feeling as well as the heady belief that he was part of a master plan that was bigger than him, a plan that had swept him up and was carrying him away. Every time he reads a story in the paper about a young couple who won an amazing all-inclusive getaway only to die in a plane crash in the middle of the ocean, or about a lottery winner who lost his millions and now relies on social security, or a young man who rams his car into a tree on his way to his wedding, Pax will see himself in the throes of naive euphoria as he hurried towards his own destruction.

Now he's slaloming along the pavement, narrowly dodging pushchairs, public benches crowded with bored teenagers, and the elderly enjoying a stroll in the warm autumn sun. He barely sees them—his body seems to be functioning independently of his mind, which remains focused on the unbelievable news that Gaspard, his agent, has just shared. Sveberg, who has come to scout settings in the French capital, has decided to add a new character to his latest screenplay. It's a secondary role, of course, but an important one nonetheless: a bartender at a luxury hotel who's happy to listen to his customers and shoulder some of their worries. Pax has just the right dose of typical French charm needed to embody the character, Gaspard explained, bragging about his privileged relationship with the director, who is known for his mercurial nature and fits of anger.

The truth is that Pax is part of a bigger deal—just a detail, really. Gaspard represents two of the film's stars. Since he gets on well with the casting director, with whom he's working on another project, he asked her to back his suggestion. Together they made a series of behind-the-scenes moves that have led to this moment.

It doesn't really matter how it happened, though. After all, everyone knows how the system works, and they all get something out of it. Pax pretends to believe Gaspard when he claims he fought hard to get him the audition. The actor knows that's far from the truth. His fifteen minutes with Sveberg haven't been "freed up" for him—he's just filling an empty block of time. He is acutely aware that his window is slim and getting slimmer by the minute; that's why he's in such a hurry. Gaspard suggested he should wear a suit, so Sveberg would "see" his character right off the bat. He said it could make all the difference. So, as soon as he hung up, Pax calculated the route from the Thea offices to his flat (twenty-five minutes), where he would throw on a suit and tie, then from his flat to the bar at the Lutetia (another twenty-five minutes).

It doesn't leave him much leeway. He should be okay if his train is held at the platform for a few minutes to regulate the service, but not if there are signalling problems or a passenger accident. He's surprised to find himself thinking this and feels bad for being such a cynic—it's unlike him. He's no idealist and no stranger to jealousy, but he's not usually this cynical. In fact, it's a regular topic of debate with his daughter, Cassandra, who makes fun of his sanguine attitude. He chastises her for her pragmatism underpinned by materialism—her cynicism, really. Cassandra argues he's too hard on her. She blames the restrictive world she lives in, claims that it's more limiting than it was for the previous generation. She suggests it's easier to be empathetic and act responsibly when you've enjoyed all the pleasures and exploited all the potential of youth. But she always ends up being the one to end the conversation, beaten by her father's eloquence, by the solid rhetoric he has perfected over years of acting, which gives him an unfair advantage.

Pax pushes his unwelcome thoughts to the back of his mind as he exits the metro and checks his watch. He's struck yet again by the contrast between the bustle at place de la Bastille, where he just was, and the calm neighbourhood he lives in, where the streets bear enchanting bucolic names— rue de l'Espérance, rue de la Providence, rue des Orchidées— but are full of small, soulless grey buildings. His mind slows for a moment in the surrounding silence, taking strength from it, like an Olympic athlete mentally preparing to wow the crowd.

In thirty-five minutes, Pax will be facing his greatest challenge. He suddenly realizes how comfortable his mediocre career has been. Until now, he's always been able to blame his middling success on an unjust system or a disappointing agent. He's let people believe he's an overlooked genius. How many times has he said, "If only I'd been given a chance"?

Well, now he has his chance. It's been handed to him on a silver platter. He hasn't been called in to audition for some small independent film or a blockbuster comedy—no, he's going to audition for Peter Sveberg. Now his situation is simple—he succeeds, or he fails. He either proves he has talent, or that he deserves the mediocre life he's been living.

The metallic caw of a raven distracts him from his musings. As he comes back to himself, he pulls out his keys, then climbs the stairs four at a time, running through the list of things to do once inside: a cool damp towel to brighten his features; cologne to mask the smell of sweat; shirt, suit, tie.

It's as he's slipping his jacket over his shoulders that he notices the noise. The banging, creaking floors and vibrating ceiling should have alerted him as soon as he came in, but concentrating on his tasks made him unaware of the world around him. Only the muffled groans and strange stomping noises finally force him to listen and to wonder what's happening on the floor above. He doesn't know anything about his neighbour, except that he or she must have moved in at the beginning of the month: he remembers seeing a "To Let" sign hanging from the window railing in August. He's never bumped into anyone on the stairs, or in the corridor or the lobby—at least not anyone he doesn't already know. He's never been bothered by any loud music. The only clue to his neighbour's identity is the handwritten name stuck slightly askew on the mailbox next to his: *A. Winckler.* Only two of the flats in the three-storey building are occupied by renters. The rest of them belong to companies. That was one of the things he had loved when he visited it the first time—the fact that it would be nearly empty in the evenings and at the weekends. Pax likes to practise his roles without dampening his enthusiasm or lowering his voice.

The noise grows louder. Furniture and bodies hit the floor. A terrible fight is going on above him. Anyone in a normal state of mind would realize something is seriously wrong, but Pax isn't in a normal state of mind—he has an imminent date with destiny. The facts and his interpretation of them are skewed by a host of inner voices. It's just a fight, he thinks, nothing big. How many screaming matches did you get into over the course of your divorce? It's really none of your business. You'd have to be pretty nosy to turn up in the middle of a private disagreement. Maybe it's not even a fight! Your imagination could just be playing tricks on you. Have you heard any insults? A cry for help? A scream, yes. But just one, and it was short. You always blow things out of proportion, develop a whole backstory for every situation ... It's an occupational hazard—actors make information and feelings their own, and then amplify them.

Pax anxiously studies his reflection in the mirror. Not too shabby: a handsome face (for an old man, as Cassandra once put it on a bad day), but a skinny body. He's never been athletic and has no experience with martial arts except for a short stint two years ago to prepare for a role as a mafia boss's right-hand man. It wasn't enough to make him feel confident about intervening, though. Fear would most likely get the best of him, making him a second victim. At the thought, his legs tremble and his heart begins to race.

"What an idiot," he reassures himself out loud. "Getting worked up like this when they're probably just moving a bed or building a dresser."

He glances ashamedly at his watch. His leeway has diminished to next to nothing with all this umming and ahhing. He has to leave now if he doesn't want to miss the last train to success. Why would he be given such an opportunity only to have it snatched away from him an hour later? He briefly considers calling the police but decides not to. He'd have to explain; maybe they'd even ask him to stay there until the officers arrived. He remembers dialling 101 a few years ago to report the theft of Cassandra's mobile phone. He waited an eternity, listening to the message "You've reached the police, please hold the line" again and again. Long enough to be murdered a hundred times. And besides, this is nothing serious, he's sure of it now. Everything's gone quiet. Totally silent. As if he dreamt it all.

It's 4.36 p.m. He locks his door and stuffs his tie in his pocket. He catches a glimpse of a man running down the stairs. Then he's gone. Pax immediately chases the image from his mind, reserving all his brain's available bandwidth for his meeting with Sveberg.

At 4.59, he walks into the Lutetia.

His slightly uneven, nervous gait conveys the blend of disarray, confusion, and excitement that consumes him. He exudes the energy of a marathon runner collapsing at the finish line, forced to concede defeat.

Peter Sveberg smiles. He's found his man.

Silence

As part of our investigation, we have received a report from the A&E doctor at [...] regarding the tests performed on Mr Alex Winckler, aged 19, on the day he was admitted. The report specifies that the victim presented with the following injuries:

* *Severe concussion resulting in a minor coma, GCS 11, temporal lobe contusion from occipital skull trauma.*
* *Multiple haematomas on the face, shoulders and thorax; open wound on the right leg.*
* *Several rib fractures on the right and left sides.*
* *Open fracture of the right tibia.*
* *Contusion of the left hand resulting in a Bennett fracture.*
* *Fracture of the right malar as well as of both orbital floors, broken nose, trauma to the soft tissue.*
* *Tear of the upper right eyelid, temporal conjunctival wound, traumatic posterior subcapsular cataract, sub-retinal haematoma, and tear of Bruch's membrane, fracture of the inner eye wall, haemorrhage of the vitreous body, in short severe trauma to the right eye, with retro-orbital haematoma and damage to the optic nerve.*

Alex's mother was the one who found him.

With no news from her son, she took the spare key to his flat and walked in to find him lying unconscious on the wooden floor, his face covered in bruises and blood, his right leg at an unnatural angle.

She crumpled without a sound.

Don't

The film will be titled *Don't*. The synopsis is already available on industry websites: *Jon recruits ten accomplices for the heist of the century, but they have no idea they're the target of a vendetta. As they move forward with the plan, they're picked off one by one.*

Matthew McConaughey is the male lead. He's the one who offloads on Pax, or rather the dark but insightful hotel bartender. Five lines, an hour of filming. McConaughey was considerate and congratulated Pax with a handshake as he left the set (unlike Sveberg, who offered an ambiguous wave). Pax felt as though the American treated him as an equal, though he's perfectly aware that it's a temporary kindness, and that McConaughey probably forgot his name as soon as the studio door closed behind him. Pax focuses on what matters—his name will be in the credits of one of next year's most anticipated releases. Once the film is in cinemas and he's added an excerpt to his showreel, his career will take off. He'll get better roles and work more often. He'll be able to leave Thea & Co., or continue to help out now and again, because he's grateful to Elizabeth for providing a decent income and being understanding these past few months. He's been awkward, late, and occasionally rude with certain clients. His appearance has changed, too. His suits are too big and he's smoking again—a habit he kicked just two years ago. The smell of stale tobacco follows him wherever he goes.

Elizabeth has no idea what really sparked this transformation. She assumes his anxiety is due to the film and the importance it holds for Pax. For the longest time he believed he would one day be a great actor, and now that dream is back on the table. She tolerates it because she sees him as proof that anything is possible—that her own trampled dreams could still become a reality. She believes Pax might still rise to fame late in his career (like Christoph Waltz who went from *Inspector Derrick* to *Inglourious Basterds*) and that she might be able to turn his success to her advantage. Wasn't McConaughey just another romcom star before he became the most wanted man in Hollywood? She's making a low-stakes bet on Pax's future.

For now, though, nothing's certain. Sveberg is still editing. Pax himself has no idea how it will turn out in the end. He'll see the film for the first time at the screening reserved for the cast and crew. And for him the stakes are higher—it's not just about his CV, it's a chance to end the war that's been going on inside his head, the question that he has been obsessing over, the question that's been eating away at him for over a year now. Success would justify his choices and his lies, and soothe the anger (which he doesn't think is egotism) that his anxiety medication struggles to keep in check.

At least he has news. Just as he slumps down into the taxi, a text message from Gaspard informs him that the cast and crew premiere will probably take place in mid-December. Elizabeth reads over his shoulder and stifles a sigh of relief. Finally, she thinks, the reward! Pax's mood has got worse since the beginning of autumn, despite persistent sunshine and temperatures nearing 25°C in October. The message is quite timely since they're en route to Demeson, a removals company whose health and safety manager is thinking about hiring Thea & Co. to do risk-management training following an accidental death. Yesterday, Elizabeth urged Pax to behave himself, fearing his agitation might have a negative impact on their potential client. Though they've never met, Elizabeth has an idea of what she's like from their email exchanges—rigorous, rigid even, which is probably an advantage when trying to make your mark in a profession dominated by men. In fact, Elizabeth had been surprised to learn that their client was a woman at all. In their first exchanges, she simply signed *E. Shimizu* and Elizabeth was convinced she was dealing with a man. When she realized her mistake, she was angry with the sexist culture that had led her to that conclusion—removals company, so necessarily a man. She couldn't believe that she—a free, independent, progressive woman running her own business—could fall into such a trap. She was also angry with herself for feeling distrustful of Emi Shimizu after visiting her page on LinkedIn (the only social network on which her name appeared) and learning she was a pretty Franco-Japanese woman in her forties with multiple degrees and a remarkable CV, as if the combination of beauty, expertise and exoticism was suspicious.

Emi Shimizu is waiting for them when they exit the lift on the eighth floor. She's wearing an old-fashioned skirt suit that goes past her knees and high heels to make up for her short stature. Her black hair is tied back in a bun adorned with two decorative fabric flowers. Her smile is disconcerting—both graceful and seemingly foreign to the lips that form it—which Pax, mistaking distance for mystery, assumes is a characteristic of her Asian origins. In truth, Emi Shimizu is at a distance from herself, but he won't learn that until much later. Elizabeth is immensely relieved when she sees Pax's respectful tone and attitude. He won't overstep the line today. In fact, he seems to be impressed, even taken with their client. Elizabeth recognizes an expression she hasn't seen on his face for over a year: that of a man—an actor—on a mission to please, to seduce, to urge Emi to look at him like she looks at no one else. He listens carefully as Ms Shimizu explains the situation. Demeson has been faced with a crisis: an employee died on the job in a lorry accident—the second such incident in six months. And perhaps it wasn't an accident at all; Christian P. may have fallen asleep at the wheel or he may have let go of it voluntarily.

Emi Shimizu lowers her voice. She clearly believes it was a suicide. She has studied the employee's case in detail. He was incredibly competent, having acquired much experience over the years, climbing the ranks from assistant mover to mover, then head mover, team manager, and finally regional manager with—she hesitates a moment—an "old-fashioned, man-to-man" leadership style based on the unspoken rules of mutual respect, keeping one's word, and hard work. In more than thirty years, Christian P. never counted his hours or complained about overwork until last spring, when the company was bought out by Demeson. It was a major opportunity, a chance to branch out internationally. Executive management invited him to a meeting with all the regional managers to announce that their methods were about to change in the best interests of all employees. They assigned young new recruits to his area, who were more demanding when it came to their working conditions and less committed to the job. He was unable to communicate with them, and they went on strike after just one week, leaving him floundering, unable to contain the situation. After that, HR offered a favourable severance package including "career transition training", but Emi is certain he felt undervalued, as if his thirty years with the company meant nothing. He felt insulted, like his very identity was being taken from him, because he was so devoted to his job that he defined himself by it. Christian P. had pulled himself up by his bootstraps and found his life's meaning in his work, and now they were shooing him out of the door, taking the piss out of him, depriving him of everything he had built. That could certainly shake a man.

In a surprising change of register, she actually says "taking the piss out of him", startling Pax and Elizabeth, though they half expect it—something shifts in her voice right before she utters the words. Then Emi Shimizu collects herself: she knows she's cast doubts on Christian P.'s intentions, but his loved ones argue he never would have deliberately harmed his two colleagues. They were injured in the accident, but not severely.

"The investigation wasn't able to determine the cause of the accident despite all of today's technical innovations?" asks Elizabeth, surprised.

Emi Shimizu focuses her gaze on the wall. She's left the room—not physically, but mentally. Her consciousness has wandered off to a faraway place where it's sifting through memories from her own life.

It's a brief, nearly imperceptible episode and now she's back and continuing with her explanation. Executive management has decided to roll out new training tools to raise awareness about psycho-social risks and safety in the workplace. As a firm believer in the virtues of theatre over PowerPoint presentations, she naturally thought of Thea & Co. She hands Pax and Elizabeth a stack of documents outlining the goals (train managers, improve instructions given to employees, improve compliance with regulations regarding good working practice and the delineation between work time and rest time). She also presents a list of job-related risks, which seems to be endless: both physical (back injury, cuts, bruises, broken bones caused by heavy lifting, falling objects, falls from heights, lorry accidents, allergies caused by dust and pollution exposure) and psychological (rude comments from stressed clients afraid their possessions might be stolen, damaged or broken, or that their windows and doors might be pulled off their hinges or their floors scratched, as well as stressful driving conditions and family difficulties stemming from the long hours).

Emi stops. Elizabeth has been taking notes. Her posture is upright and reassuring—that of an experienced business-woman who has all the answers.

"There's one more thing," adds Ms Shimizu. "Working as a mover is seen as an odd job that even an idiot can do as long as they're strong enough. It's a thankless job that people accept because they can't find anything better, because they're not qualified for anything else. It's important to take their frustration, their wounded self-esteem and their feelings of marginalization into consideration."

Pax sits up with a start. Emi's looking at him; in fact she's been staring at him for several minutes. She feels like he understands everything, absolutely everything she's ex-plained: Christian P. and the need for training at Demeson, but also her world view and her own fears, which somehow slipped into her monologue. She noticed the way Pax looked unable to catch his breath when she mentioned the movers' struggle with shattered ideals, frustration, and feelings of worthlessness, while Elizabeth remained emotionless, focused on her tablet. Emi didn't expect this. She didn't expect to feel the sensation growing quietly in her stomach, rousing and shaking off the layers of self-protection that until now have muffled and muted her pain. She didn't expect this chaos in her heart, the feverish wave spreading to all of her organs. Her turmoil overflows and reaches Pax as a silent conversation begins between them, but she cuts it short by standing up to distract herself from her sudden fascination. A sixth sense warns her that this man is danger-ous. She doesn't have time or space in her life for a relation-ship, be it sensual, sexual or emotional.

Elizabeth stands in turn to conclude the meeting. She already has several training modules and tools in mind that are suitable for the situation. She even offers a "money-back guarantee"—she loves to throw in overused consumerist slogans. It takes clients by surprise and it works every time. She noticed Emi's fascination with Pax and is delighted. Another reason for the client to sign the contract. Tonight she'll send Ms Shimizu a quote, being sure to add that Pax will run the training. Tomorrow she'll receive approval and the down payment, and they'll schedule it in the calendar. A perfectly executed deal, just how she likes them. It should put Thea & Co. squarely in the black for the year.

As Emi escorts them back to the lift, Pax notices that a strand of dark hair has escaped from her bun and is delicately caressing the back of her neck. He finds it charming, extraordinary even—two adjectives that had disappeared from his vocabulary. He remembers Gaspard's text message and feels like his life is suddenly back on the rails, like a rusted old engine stored in a forgotten shed that suddenly comes to life. As soon as he steps outside, he dials Cassandra's number, surprised by how happy he feels. He wants to invite her to dinner, talk to her about the film, tell her yet again about how encouraging Matthew was—they're on first-name terms when he talks about the actor to his daughter or Elizabeth.

On her way back to her office, Emi Shimizu catches a glimpse of her reflection in a mirror. Her bun has come loose, and an escaped strand trails down her neck into the stiff collar of her shirt. She stops abruptly. Every morning she goes through the same steps, in the same order, to tie back her long hair and adorn the bun with flowers. Every day she comes to work wearing the same outfit: a skirt suit that she has in several different shades of grey, and a round-neck coat—a woollen one in the winter and a cotton one in the summer. She always takes the same route, always steps onto the stairs with her right foot first, always orders the daily special at the canteen, and always uses the same notebooks and black markers, which she orders in boxes from the stationery department. Her impeccable and unchanging appearance commands respect—it's her suit of armour. No one can see the shy, sensitive child or the young woman full of hope she once was. Emi Shimizu wears the impenetrable uniform of the disenchanted and has no plans to discard it.

She quickly removes a pin from her bun, takes hold of the loose strand, twists it, and secures it back in its proper place.

Takeno

Emi Shimizu is pale, as if she were sculpted from limestone and coated in a fine layer of tears and rain.

Before, as the train left behind skyscrapers and hurried past industrial zones, her face would light up with an ethereal glow at the sight of the maple, beech, oak, birch and chestnut trees that lined the tracks in increasing numbers between stations. When she stepped off the train, her gaze focused on the swaying canopy of the neighbouring forest; her body seemed ready to fly. She would take the back exit, which was just a hundred metres or so from the edge of the wood and was dotted with bushes and undergrowth. She would stop, breathe in the wild smells, and gracefully dart across the road like a nervous doe looking for a safe place to hide. She always found her way easily in places where others would have been trapped by brambles. She would carefully circumnavigate heather, burdock and nightshade, violets and lily of the valley in spring, penny buns and puffball mushrooms in the autumn. She would linger a few minutes, eyes closed, stroking the bark of the trees, feeling the soft earth beneath her black ankle boots. This proximity to nature restored her inner balance, like a rush of endorphins that instantly filled all the cracks in her existence and left her feeling whole and healed.

But the ritual disappeared a year ago, replaced by a constant race against time. Emi struggles without it—more than anyone could ever imagine. She has rediscovered the cruel sensation that something is always missing, which tormented her throughout childhood and her teen years, when she was suffocated by the smells of petrol, soldering, and exhaust in the garage and by those of new plastic, synthetic fragrances, and bad coffee in the showroom. Sounds plague her now. The clinking of the train as it changes tracks, the sound of rubber on tarmac, shrieking alarms, shouting people on foot or on bikes, drivers, delivery men— all of it takes her back to the family dealership, with the persistent din of engines and steel alongside squeaking, sanding, banging, and twisting tools, and above it all her mother's voice directing the team like the head of a commando unit.

She takes refuge in the few memories she has of her first trip to Japan, where her father took her to meet her grandparents. She remembers walking in blinding sunlight towards the village until they reached their house, which seemed tiny compared to hers. She remembers the elation she felt on the beach, a cove nestled between two hills, a feeling heightened by the exuberant vegetation in shades of green and bronze, and the calm aquamarine water. She remembers the steps she climbed silently through the woods to the temple, holding her grandfather's hand, and the modesty of the women who sat on the sand beneath large white tents. The rift that continues to tear her apart today began that summer, in Takeno. She fell hopelessly in love with the serene natural environment and the dignified, reserved people with slanted eyes like hers—eyes that had incited nothing but teasing since she'd started school. She begged her father to stay longer, to move them to Japan, where she suddenly felt at home. Izuru pursed his lips tightly, like the clams they had collected in the rockpools, to keep in the words an eight-year-old girl wouldn't understand. He simply shook his head sadly, hiding his bitterness and concentrating on his fatherly role of giving Emi a chance to cherish happy memories of her grandparents. Just a few weeks later, she learned her grandfather had died.

Then, the next year, her grandmother passed away. The trip to Takeno had been more than a reunion—it had been goodbye.

Emi is forty-four years old now, and she figured out the inescapable logic that has weighed down her family and created this exhausting feeling of dissonance long ago. It all began years before her birth, when a schism opened between her father and his parents because Izuru had chosen to leave Honda's headquarters in Hamamatsu to go and work at the plant in Belgium, and then he had gone on to marry Sonia. The brilliant engineer destined for a lofty career had fallen in love with the daughter of a French motorbike dealer visiting Aalst on business. Quite a fall indeed in the eyes of Issey and Akiko Shimizu—a hospital manager and a librarian at the Toyooka municipal library respectively. They refused to attend the wedding or even to meet their daughter-in-law. They wrote to Izuru: *You have stolen our dream*, alluding to Soichiro Honda's motto, "We must always pursue our dreams", which Izuru had painted on his wall when he was still a hard-working student with excellent marks. They could not see what drew their son to Sonia. She listened to psyche-delic rock, smoked pot, and rode motorbikes that weighed more than she did. She was equally talented as a guitar player, a motorbike rider, and a mechanic. She had posed for an ad campaign regally perched on a CB750 in a leather one-piece, stealing the spotlight—and soon the reins of the company—from her astounded father. She embodied spontaneity, desire, movement and wonder, while Izuru, with his passion for numbers and philosophy, was charming in his own way, thanks to the allure of the unusual and inscrutable. They seemed incompatible, but their differences turned out to be complementary. Yoko Ono had married John Lennon just a few months before Izuru and Sonia met and, though they didn't realize it, the famous couple played a decisive role in the powerful attraction that drew them together and never faded, triumphing over the pessimistic predictions of everyone around them.

Emi Shimizu was born of this unique and self-sufficient entity. It was her destiny to disappoint both her parents, because she could never be both the *In* and the *Yô*. As a child, she wasn't interested in motorbikes or maths. She was a good student, but not excellent. She lacked confidence and wit, particularly when faced with her classmates, who repeated the xenophobic things they heard on the news at a time when Japan was felt to be an economic enemy. But even if she'd had the courage to speak up, she wouldn't have known what to say—her features were Asian, but since her father had chosen assimilation over integration (due largely to his parents' rejection), her culture was entirely French. She grew up with the suffocating feeling that she was inadequate and ill-suited to her environment, torn between the fanciful expectations of her parents, teachers, and other children. Takeno was the first place she ever felt truly at peace, thanks to the contact with nature which marked her so deeply that it created a Pavlovian response. Now, whenever she walks on grass, touches, or even just contemplates trees, she feels centred for a moment. She draws her immense strength from this initiatory trip: at the age of eight, she confronted her solitude and made peace with her lost illusions. She gave up on winning more of her mother's attention, more flexibility from her father, or more sincerity and selflessness from anyone. She accepted that she would always be a *hafu*—a term she heard on her second trip to Japan at the age of twenty, when she learned she would always be foreign, wherever she lived. It didn't break her, though. She possesses surprising energy and strength for someone with floating roots. She can be bent but never felled. Though she sometimes slows in the wind or when she comes up against a wall, she keeps her eyes on the horizon, adjusting her path and her goals to fit whatever changes life throws at her. This unique ability has saved her from the abyss many times and continues to do so today.

Langlois, the psychologist who has been seeing Emi since her son was attacked, is constantly surprised. As the father of a child the same age as Alex, he wonders if he could survive a similar situation, even with all his years of schooling and clinical experience. The incident has shaken him, partly because he can't help but identify with her, but also because of the questions it raises. He's mentioned it a few times at dinners out (without revealing any details, of course; he's an ethical man). The media covered the story closely for several days: the young man was handsome, unassuming, well liked. A model citizen whom someone had attacked without leaving a trace. There had been no sign of a break-in and nothing had been stolen. The shock and horror displayed by his fellow diners were clear evidence that the incident was a phenomenon that had touched all of society. It's not just about the victim and his circle. It's a totally random, unprovoked attack that kindles widespread feelings of rampant danger. It's the unthinkable idea that anything can happen at any time, that no one is safe, not even our children. That said, the nagging doubt that people cling to—believing nothing is ever *truly* unprovoked, that there's always a motive—is hardly more reassuring. The betrayal of the social contract, the wilful breaking of the law, is even more disturbing than the unprecedented level of violence. The psychologist is worried. He's recently noticed among his patients, as well as in the behaviour of the general population, media messages and the rise of extremist politics, a silent, gradual destabilization that has exacerbated individualism and made people more distrustful of others and of the unknown. He can't help but feel that fear, madness and violence are all growing more intense, even though he's perfectly aware of the bias created by the twenty-four-hour news cycle, which often lacks rigour and impartiality. Deep down, he's convinced that these symptoms are not proof of an inexorable decline, but of the necessary restructuring of a world subjected to the positive and negative effects of technology, which cannot be contained, and whose acceleration leads to dangerous mistakes. But none of that resolves the problem of individual suffering. We must all find a way to survive our own personal dramas. As must Emi Shimizu, who turns up at every appointment carefully coiffed and made up to speak in a monotone devoid of apparent emotion, though she seems to be fully present. The psychologist wonders how she manages to walk through the hurricane, how she can remain upright in her situation. Though he believed at first that it was a façade which would eventually crumble to let her deeply buried wounds show through, he now knows he was wrong. Emi Shimizu seems to have built invisible and mysterious ramparts around herself that enable her to fulfil her self-imposed mission.

She's sitting across from him now at their bi-monthly appointment on the edge of her seat, seemingly refusing its comfort. Nothing has really changed since they last saw one another, but he notices that twice during the session she seems to be elsewhere, which is unusual. He assumes she's preoccupied by her complex daily life and tells her how much he admires her. Getting ordinary things done each day for the past thirteen months, isn't that extraordinary? He uses the word *hero*. Emi is disconcerted, feels Langlois is flattering her, and dismisses the term. Heroes are brave, while she feels she is driven alternately by fear, necessity, duty and love—not by courage. The psychologist gives in. Emi records the date of their next session in her mobile and shakes his hand with a slight smile that is little more than a reflex, a piece of her armour, that leaves Langlois satisfied though vaguely troubled.

It's 8.30 p.m. and completely dark by the time she reaches her building. Warm light emanates from the windows at this time of the evening. Most of her neighbours are home, pans on the hob, tables set, children in bed.

Courage, she thinks as she inserts the key into the lock and listens to the sound of canned laughter on a TV gameshow, would be discussing his future with Alex. His dream has been stolen and there's no hope of getting it back.

Courage would be accepting her own despair in order to try and move on from it. It would be letting herself live, letting the unexpected emotions stirred in her by Pax Monnier this afternoon spread and grow.

Courage would be abandoning the fruitless thoughts of vengeance and hatred. There is no one to punish, no one to hate.

It's still invisible

Their meeting is scheduled for Friday at 4.30 p.m. Pax suggested a few slots earlier in the week, arguing it would be best to handle the situation as quickly as possible to keep the Christian P. incident from influencing too many employees. Moving quickly will prove the company's commitment and how highly it values its employees, he argued to justify his haste in an email to Emi. It's the best way to defuse difficult questions. She chose the last date in the list, claiming her schedule was completely booked. They're both lying, but do they even realize it? Emi Shimizu's graceful body and face have been scared onto Pax's retinas since the day they met, to the point that her image sometimes overrides reality. He wants to see her again, whatever the cost. He wants to experience that feeling he'd given up on, the energy radiating from his lower abdomen. But more than anything, he wants the chance to escape his anxiety again. Even as he shook her hand and stepped into the lift, he began thinking about the email he would send her, working on different strategies depending on whether she accepted or refused the quote.

Emi Shimizu signed the contract. She wants to move quickly as well, but not *too* quickly. She realizes how serious the situation is: the number of employees on sick leave has been abnormally high at Demeson since Christian P.'s death. She remembers the hurtful, cutting remarks she once heard about her job (she's not a "money-maker", she costs the company a lot), but now her role is crucial. She's responsible for rekindling the employees' trust in the company and helping them turn the page. It's a critical moment in her career. And yet, this inner turmoil has somehow taken hold, penetrating her mind and corrupting its functioning. Something she cannot describe has taken control. She's disoriented when she thinks about Pax Monnier, about what she saw in his eyes; even more so when she thinks of the sensory storm that carried her off like a tiny pebble caught in a wave. She's doing her best to ignore it, but everything—a breeze across her shoulders, the heat of the laptop on her knees, or the open window—keeps bringing her back to this paradoxical feeling which she desires and fears in equal measure. She accepts that she may simply be the victim of biological and hormonal processes, that it may be down to age or frustration. She hasn't had a man in her life for a good ten years, but she hasn't missed it either. Sometimes, she hears snatches of conversations in the corridors, near the coffee machine, or at the stationery cupboard. The employees mostly talk about sex and affairs, making fun of colleagues—men or women—who they assume no longer have a sex life. They seem to believe it's a sign of failure, of a hopeless, wasted existence. They never talk about her, though. She has everyone fooled without even trying—her beauty and impeccable appearance lead them to believe she's skilled in the art of seduction when in fact, they're just part of the fortress she's constantly strengthening.

Could her inner turmoil simply be due to unsatisfied urges? She's considered the possibility, but doesn't believe it, at least not as the sole explanation. She may be incendiary, but Pax wouldn't have been the first spark—Demeson is full of more virile men. She would already have caught fire. No. What's made the difference and begun to break through her fortifications is the inescapable feeling that she and Pax

Monnier have a shared fate, or perhaps a shared past; not in the literal sense, of course, because she's never seen him before, not even as an actor (she never watches TV), but in terms of life experiences. She realized it the first time they met—this man knows the depths of the abyss. This vague feeling is persistent, overwhelming, transformative. That's why she chose Friday evening: to give herself time to get herself together. And—not that she'd admit this was a factor in her decision—the offices will be nearly empty then as well. No one will be around to interrupt her or ask her to sign something. She'll have plenty of time.

They're sitting across from one another, both as far back in their chairs as possible, fighting the same combination of awkwardness and attraction. Pax is more comfortable, though. His acting talents help him face most situations. Whenever he feels a rush of adrenaline coming on, he thinks about Cassandra's mother, which provokes a cold anger capable of putting out any fire. Emi flips through the Christian P. file. Seeing his jovial face with his forehead wrinkled from too much laughter followed by too much suffering reminds her of her priorities—though they may be unable to shed light on the circumstances of his death, they must do everything they can to significantly improve safety conditions and prevent any future "accidents".

"The training is designed to be fun," explains Pax. "That's our secret. Make them laugh and play. Surprise them to teach them, like we do with children."

They'll need to be able to hold the attention of a distracted audience, always pleased to escape the daily routine, but quick to fall asleep. There will be two actors on stage—one who follows the rules (Number 1), and one who couldn't care less (Number 2), who is obviously more popular, because he embodies a combination of freedom, defiance, insolence and charisma. There will be straightforward and sarcastic jokes, a bit of light slapstick, and some interaction for the participants. In short, it'll be a real show.

Pax has written (or really just adapted a scenario Thea has already used a hundred times) a dialogue featuring different constraints and rules. He gives it to Emi to read. As she turns the pages, the story becomes more serious. It becomes clear that Number 2's nonchalance hides a lack of rigour, professionalism and confidence. Number 2 turns out to be no more than a funny but incompetent amateur. Then the accident happens.

"At exactly the same time," explains Pax, who has a gift for the tragicomic, "an ambulance siren will blare, stopping the audience in their tracks—people who were laughing just minutes before, when Number 2 mocked Number 1's straight-laced nature. Believe me, Emi, we'll be able to hear a pin drop!"

He uses her first name: a subtle manoeuvre to get closer to her, a test. She doesn't seem to notice. He continues his speech. "The ultimate twist comes when Number 1 sticks to rules that no longer suit the situation, doesn't ask for help and wastes precious time, complicating the work of the paramedics. The scene emphasizes the importance of following the rules, but also paying attention to others' behaviour, working together, and thinking like a team."

Emi shifts her head back slightly in a pensive posture. A thin gold chain gracefully follows the peaks of her collarbones. It must have borne a pendant once upon a time. Did she lose it? Remove it? She's not wearing a wedding ring or any other jewellery.

"A shift away from individuals for a more collective look at safety," she muses out loud. "Looking to restore all the links in the chain of causality. But does that chain even have a beginning or an end? Who should be included in it? The manager who asked employees to carry out impossible assignments, or the employee who accepted them despite his sciatica? The doctor who failed to notice the toll work was taking on his patient, or the lover who failed to see his worsening exhaustion? The company's bonus policy, which rewards overtime, or a difficult divorce wreaking havoc on the mind? The HR team, which has rolled changes out too quickly, or unemployment rates? The pouring rain, which reduced visibility for Christian P. the night his lorry crashed?"

"I'm with you. The idea of responsibility is a farce. It doesn't resolve anything at all."

He goes quiet, surprised by the shameless boldness of his words. He suddenly feels like a tiny, easily overlooked, useless spot at the centre of a huge void. Why did he improvise like that?

He's afraid he's shocked her, but Emi Shimizu simply nods. "Even if we could outline the limits," she continues, "we'll never be able to foresee everything. We can't protect every situation with rules, procedures, good intentions and altruism. However carefully a driver follows the Highway Code, she may not be able to avoid hitting a child running after a ball. Chance, sudden changes and improbable events don't follow rules." She takes a deep breath, her eyes half closed. "Life is risky."

Her narrow chest is suddenly as perfectly still as a statue. Her gaze drifts, then disappears beyond the walls of the room—just like it did the first time they met, Pax notes disconcertedly. Has she left her body? He looks up involuntarily, as if he might see her glued to the ceiling. How silly. What he knows for certain is that Emi Shimizu is elsewhere, far out of reach. She's moving deeper into the murky waters of her own memory. It isn't about Christian P., it's about her inability to protect those she loves from the unpredictable.

After a few seconds she's turned so pale she looks dead, mummified even. Unsure what has stolen her attention, Pax assumes Christian P.'s death has seriously affected her. Were they just colleagues? Or friends? Lovers? This thought leads straight on to another one, an indescribable blend of jealousy, desire and compassion. He wants to bring this woman back to life, hold her close, give her back the life she's deprived herself of. He doesn't realize how presumptuous this is, nor what it reveals about his own troubles and torments. He's filled with a new energy which pushes back the darkness. The words rush out, the combined result of dozens of his past roles as consoling characters—lawyers, therapists, fathers, sons, brothers and confidants. He talks to her about uncertainty, the clay from which life is sculpted and the mother of all fears, which limits, confines and suffocates him as well. The colour slowly returns to Emi's cheeks.

She's back—and even better, she's smiling.

"Maybe we have to accept uncertainty," she whispers. "Maybe that's what it means to be brave."

He nods and smiles in turn. Their eyes meet for a second, then they quickly look away. Later, they'll be able to identify the precise moment when their relationship shifted. It's still invisible, but it's all there, in their shared smile. They've crossed a boundary from which there is no return. The conversation turns back to the training—technical details, costs, scheduling. On Tuesday, Pax will take Emi to visit the convention centre that will host the participants, and then they'll work together to perfect the dialogue and finalize the sessions. It's easy to say goodbye, since they know they'll be seeing each other again soon.

As he leaves Emi's office building, Pax is struck by the depth of the darkness that envelops the city, dotted with lit windows that look like tiny gold sequins. It's late. He texts Elizabeth: *Productive meeting. We got on well.*

Emi Shimizu is up to date on all her open files. She could go home, but she remains at her desk, her back straight, hands resting on her lap. She listens to the silence, wishing it could last forever.

But her phone vibrates with a message from an impatient Alex.

Dallas Buyers Club

They make love three weeks after their first meeting. Pax invited Emi to come out for a drink after the session reserved for the company's most senior employees (they've formed six groups, which will be trained one at a time over the following weeks). Since some of them—friends of Christian P.—had a negative attitude towards the training, Pax felt they should make some adjustments right away, and Emi immediately agreed to meet.

Together they choose a terrace surrounded by trees. It's almost empty and there are blankets on all the chairs. The outdoor heat lamps cast a red glow on them, enhancing the intimate atmosphere. The waiter is discreet when he takes their order. Pax will have a Martini, Emi a glass of Sancerre. She hesitates—it's been so long since she's been to a bar or a café. She doesn't know the rules. With no habits to fall into, she has to improvise. He gulps down half his glass at once, but she drinks slowly, sip by sip, like someone edging cautiously down a poorly lit path.

They finish the changes quickly and the conversation drifts. Emi asks Pax about his profession. She's not interested in his talent, his ability to slip into someone else's skin, the different roles he's played, films he's been in, or even the highs and lows of the ego roller coaster. She wants to know more about how he handles the intermittent nature of his job, the uncertainty.

"How can you live with such ... instability?" she asks, choosing her words carefully.

Pax thinks about his answer. When he chose his path at the age of seventeen, he had no idea what lay ahead. He was convinced that he'd soon be a star. He had a pure—read naive—vision of what it meant to be an actor. He thought it was all about the work, about art, or even genius for a select few. And he thought he was pretty talented. His secondary school drama teacher had described his final performance as "memorable". At the time, Pax was still considering studying law, but that one word gave him the courage to stand up to his parents, who were worried about his future.

Not long after, a friend who was in the same theatre classes as Pax suggested the comment may not have been a compliment. The teacher was known for his sarcasm and overuse of irony. Pax could have been unsettled by this revelation, but he somehow managed to blunt the impact by ending their friendship. Would a real friend suggest such a thing? Would a real friend call his talent into question? And even if he did, wouldn't a real friend keep such deeply hurtful suppositions to himself? Ironically, the scene in question had been from *The Misanthrope*, a play in which hypocrisy plays a major role. Pax had delivered his lines with a certain flair that day: "What, I, your friend? Go strike that off your books. / I have professed to be so hitherto; / But after seeing what you did just now / I tell you flatly I am so no longer / And want no place in such corrupted hearts." In the end, rather than slow his progress, the insult propelled him forward.

But Pax doesn't realize any of this. It would be hard for him to admit that he made such an important decision out of pride. Even so, he still occasionally Googles the name of that "friend" to make sure he's still forgotten (he had his time in the spotlight twenty years ago in a musical), that his career is dead and cannot be resuscitated.

Pax doesn't know how to free himself from his past. He

often looks back at his youth and berates himself for being so blind. He didn't know he needed to cultivate his image and build a network to have a successful career. He didn't notice the walls rising up around him. He didn't make the right friends, something that catapulted others—who weren't necessarily any better than him—to stardom, with all the accompanying tabloid fame. He accepted whatever roles were offered to him because he had to pay his bills, because he was flattered someone was interested, and because he saw it as a chance to gain experience. He played in trivial productions, wasting his time, because he had forgotten that while great roles reveal talent, talent cannot make any role great. He neglected the importance of kindling desire, that fleeting combination of rarity, quality, and ambition. As a result, he developed a reputation as an entirely unexceptional actor, and prestigious casting directors pushed his applications aside with disdain. Pax Monnier, no thank you. His disloyal friend's allegation turned out to be quite prophetic.

That said, Pax has rarely been out of work. He knows how to get the job done, and his regular, reassuring form of beauty is in high demand in television. TV series love to promote familiar faces viewers can easily identify with. And his distinctive voice has brought in quite a few voiceover contracts. So he may cry tears of rage and hate when he learns he's not even longlisted for illustrious projects, and now doubts he'll ever gain widespread recognition and glory, but he's never had to deal with the anxiety of failing to make ends meet. His earnings dipped only once, when the series he starred in was cancelled after thirteen seasons. Happily, that was precisely when Elizabeth asked him to join Thea & Co.

So emotional instability, perhaps. Technical, practical and financial instability however, no. But why destroy the illusion?

"Well, instability is the biggest challenge," he lies. "Everyone knows that art demands sacrifice, but the rewards are worth it. We live intense parallel lives and get to rub shoulders with great talents!"

He segues into *Don't*. Since the beginning of the conversation, he's been feverishly awaiting an opportunity to talk about shooting the film, to drop the names that are guaranteed to impress two or three generations. He knows Emi isn't a movie lover or into film stars, but he can see she's enjoying learning about a new field. He watches as her posture softens, her shoulders relax, and her chin drops slightly. If he knew her better (but does anyone really know her?), he'd realize just how momentous this shift is. Emi Shimizu has just unlocked an armoured door that has been sealed for over a year. Her entire being splits open as Pax enthusiastically talks about Sveberg's brilliance and mood swings, then about "Matthew's" style and panache. He describes his "relationship" with the actor, praising his wisdom and quoting him from memory: "If it's happiness you're after, you'll be let down a lot, and you'll often be unhappy. But joy is something else entirely."

If the quote had come from anyone else, the conversation would have ended right there. Emi would have seen it as a terrible cliché, one of those trite truisms that are spouted again and again by "well-being professionals". But since it's Matthew McConaughey, that changes everything: Alex was sixteen when they went to see *Dallas Buyers Club*. She can no longer remember why she went with him—a friend of his must have cancelled at the last minute. She regrets the fact that her memories are so muddled. She wishes she had recorded every detail of their time together, wishes she'd thought to take a picture of her son that day, and every other day until 23 September last year. She wishes she had preserved all his expressions and his unmaimed face. The images and feelings she had thought were permanent, the ones that prompted waves of indescribable love, year after year, but have now begun to fade, replaced by reality. Now all that's left are fragments floating aimlessly through the abyss of her memory, which only rarely come to the surface, summoned by a sound or a word. And that is what's happened now: McConaughey. She sees herself walking down the street with Alex, hears the timbre and tone of his voice, his enthusiasm about the actor's talent and the deep meaning of the story. Ron Woodroof, the violent, macho, homophobic cowboy who gets AIDS and finds out he only has a month to live, but decides to fight, to go on a lone crusade against pharmaceutical lobbies, on a quest for treatments other than AZT. Woodroof has to give up on the world he thought he knew, but his struggles teach him about humanity, tolerance and respect—and help extend the lives of thousands of people, including himself.

As they walked, Alex picked up the pace, driven by a sense of euphoria. It suddenly seemed like anything was possible, like everyone could shape their fate if they were strong enough. Emi admired her son and in that moment, she loved him more than anything. They haven't been to the cinema together since. The opportunity never presented itself—the stars have to align to get a teenager to go out with his parents.

Then the universe created a black hole.

"My son really likes Matthew McConaughey."

"So you have children?"

Pax has been dying to ask this question. He's wondered about Emi Shimizu's family a hundred times. Since he divorced Cassandra's mother, whom he once loved as much as he hates her now, he hasn't had any real relationships. Whether the women he sees are married or not, mothers or not, doesn't matter as long as they bolster his faith in his sexual prowess. They all seem identical to him, figures in a crowd: tall or short, blonde, brunette, ginger, curly hair or straight, thin or curvy, light or dark skin; they all dress, walk, think, speak and live in the same way—the way magazines and social networks tell them to, erasing all meaningful differences. He jumps from one to the next without getting attached. It would have been easy to leave his usual milieu to find something new, but he never dared. He met them all on sets, in television offices or production firms, popular restaurants or cafés, places he heard about from friends or that popped up on his phone. He preferred to keep swimming through this disappointingly homogenous aquarium, blending perfectly into the shoal of male actors with his carefully tended three-day beard and fashionable suits. He knowingly engaged in these mediocre relationships to punish himself for the failure of his one real relationship, for which he blames himself. But for the past year, for other reasons, he hasn't been with anyone at all.

Meeting Emi Shimizu sparked something new in him. Would he have been able to appreciate the full extent of her beauty if he hadn't first fallen so low? He was drowning when she came into his life. She was completely different from every other woman he knew—powerful and yet vulnerable. After just a few work sessions spent at a desk, discussing choices of words and gestures, and subconsciously sharing their opinions on life's difficulties, he was convinced that she would pull him out of the mire that was suffocating him. Now he wants to make sure she'll never let go of his hand again, that he means as much to her as she does to him. But is she even single?

"I have a son. He's twenty. And you?"

"My daughter is twenty-four. I've been divorced for years," he quickly explains.

"Me too."

They breathe deeply as they both imagine parallels between their stories. In reality their paths are dissimilar, if not complete opposites. Their marriages weren't based on the same premise and didn't end for the same reasons. Alex's father, Christophe, fell in love with a family, a clan—the noisy world of mechanics and the glorious queen who reigned over it. He was one of those falsely rebellious young men, a lazy opportunist. He was laid-back and charming but spent most of his time haunting the cafés around the Sorbonne rather than attending his classes there, where he met Emi. He dreamed of travelling to the United States, of seeing the world, and had pinned a poster from *Vanishing Point* (featuring the dazzling Gilda Texter perched naked on a red-and-white Honda CB350, her hair in the wind) to his wall. The first time he ever came to the dealership and got a glimpse of the poster of Sonia on her 750 was a revelation. More than anything else in the world, he wanted to be part of that family, which was so much more exciting than his own. His parents were mortgage brokers who lived a quiet life in their three-bedroom apartment in Paris's 17th arrondissement—the nice part, they always specified, as if there were an invisible border protecting them from another less tasteful neighbour-hood—and a little house on the sea in Dinard. They had, of course, purchased both of them well below market value. He imagined himself riding a powerful motorbike like Peter Fonda in *Easy Rider* (a film Sonia showed him) and convinced himself he was attracted to Emi, whom he watched carefully when he wasn't focused on his future in-laws. He convinced her, too. She'd only had one boyfriend, at the age of fifteen, with whom she'd done little more than kiss. She was uncom-fortable with her short stature and nearly flat chest at a time when the five-foot-ten-inch Eva Herzigova was on every bill-board with her smoky eyes and heaving breasts. Her time in secondary school had made her distrustful (several different boys had charmed her and taken advantage of her naivety to get discounts on their mopeds), and her first years at university hadn't been much better. She'd felt lost in the crowded lecture theatres, where, after spending an hour and a half on the train, in the metro and on a bus, she always had to sit on the stairs for lack of any free seats. She would have liked to make friends, to be a part of the noisy groups that ran down the corridors laughing, but she didn't know how to go about it. Christophe came into her life at just the right time, standing behind her in an endless line as they waited to finalize their enrolment for the semester. He was instantly drawn to her Asian features, the way she held her head, and her enigmatic grace. Our fate often hinges on the little things: Emi's file was incomplete. She needed an envelope in a particular size, and Christophe just happened to have an extra. He swapped it for her promise to have coffee with him. Emi had chosen to study psychology, despite a bitter confrontation with her father, who considered the social sciences to be an incomprehensible oxymoron. Christophe was studying law and political science. He delivered stirring utopian speeches with an elegance and charm that soon earned him Sonia's attention (and a fair dose of suspicion from Izuru). Their relationship followed the usual course. Christophe's parents invested in a studio and let them live there. It was tiny, but had a lovely balcony that faced south, where Emi planted and tended to evergreen shrubs and seasonal flowers. She'd just received a first in her master's degree in psychology when she found out she was pregnant. Christophe had repeated a year twice, more interested in his passionate but fruitless discussions about the state of the world than in studying for exams. He had only just managed to pull it together and earn his bachelor's degree. He saw Emi's pregnancy as a way out. He officially gave up on his studies and joined his family's brokerage firm. Emi was no longer quite so in love, but she couldn't say it out loud. Since they'd moved in together, she'd felt freer than she ever had before. On Sunday she sometimes let Christophe visit Sonia and Izuru on his own while she studied for her exams and savoured the solitude, the silence filled with her thoughts and dreams that intertwined deliciously. She thought the baby would fix things. Though the child wasn't planned, he had been wanted since the beginning of his existence in utero, and that kept growing while her love for Christophe silently faded away.

Everything had changed for Christophe as well. He was stuck in a terrible dilemma: he refused to leave this family (or rather Sonia and the garage, where he liked to spend entire days), but he was tired of Emi. Her relative success highlighted his failure. He'd not only given up on his studies, but also turned his back on his ideals—all that was left of them was the *Vanishing Point* poster, which now hung in the loo. Most people would have identified these changes as the usual transition from adolescence to adulthood, which dampens so many revolutionary spirits, but Christophe felt belittled and worthless. His libido was at an all-time low. Like Emi, he hoped it was only a phase. He ignored his desire when a delightful tingling sensation took hold of him as he met with a pretty client one warm spring day. Something between him and Emi had broken, but instead of ending their relationship, they let themselves get carried away by their circumstances. They got married right after Alex was born. Emi selected a short excerpt from *Nuptials* by Albert Camus to be read at the wedding: "Weddings often end this way—entire lives pledged to each other through an exchange of mint sweets." The attendees found it adorable—entire lives! No one thought about how terrifying those two words could be. Emi and Christophe were married for fifteen years. Their sex life was nearly non-existent, but no one ever would have guessed it. They lived together peacefully, leaving each other alone and tacitly accepting the possibility of extramarital affairs. They moved into a bigger apartment and raised their son together. He was a happy, easy-going little boy, whose early gift for maths and physics delighted his maternal grandfather. Christophe had a few flings, but nothing meaningful, until a new financial advisor named Pauline began working at the firm. She sparked new ambitions. That same year, Sonia and Izuru sold the dealership and went to live in the south of France. They of course had no idea, but this decision tipped the scales. Christophe finally felt he was free of an imaginary contract and told Emi he wanted a divorce. She asked him to wait until Alex had finished the school year. They hired the same barrister—the father of one of Alex's schoolmates. He was a funny, educated man who instantly fell under Emi's spell. Before the ink was even dry on the divorce papers, he took her to dinner. Like Christophe before him, he was in the right place at the right time. He was married and had no intention of leaving his wife, which was ideal for Emi, who was in no hurry to commit. They saw each other for six months. She fell for him and was surprised to find she lusted after his body, his smell, his voice. She came in his arms and couldn't believe she had mistaken pleasure for an orgasm all those years. He suddenly mattered to her—enough for her to struggle with him ending their relationship. Luckily her inner shield protected her from any real sadness. Emi doesn't know it, but she could have fallen truly in love, like her parents had, if he hadn't ended it. This unexpected episode taught her that with Christophe, she hadn't experienced even a sliver of what a woman might hope to feel. Neither the physical ecstasy nor the emotional passion. Her affair with the barrister sowed a seed in her that has been growing silently ever since, a powerful longing, which she suppresses for fear of what it might become. She began hiding behind Alex, devoting most of her time to him even before the assault, and even more so now. But she's still a wild field made fertile by years of lying fallow. Her misfortunes have only pushed back the life force growing within her, which is now poised to erupt.

In many ways, Pax Monnier has followed the opposite path. There were fireworks when he first met Sara, a new student in his acting class. Her short hair was dyed bright red and she had a biomechanical tattoo on the back on her neck. Though that sort of thing is common now, at the time it lent her a sensual warrior allure that made her stand out. Pax looked a bit like Joe Strummer and was always wearing a leather jacket he'd decorated with the Clash's *Give 'Em Enough Rope* album cover. Their passion knocked them both sideways—nothing else would ever equal its intensity. They weren't teenagers any more, but they weren't quite adults either. With their fiery personalities, they kept playing the impassioned heroes they embodied on stage in their real lives. They loved, hurt, betrayed, left, humiliated and challenged each another again and again, trapped in the vortex they'd created. It was a spectacular form of catharsis that was far beyond their comprehension. Then Sara, who followed her every whim (she later discovered she was bipolar; fortunately lithium helped her to manage it), decided to quit her acting and foreign language studies for a job in a big travel agency, where she would travel the world on the lookout for new hotels to market. Pax got a recurring role in a primetime TV show. They got married when they were just twenty and twenty-two years old, without any family or friends, on a beach on Kythira, the birthplace of Aphrodite. This was Sara's idea—she was more invested in building their legend than in living it. Things could have become calmer between them since Pax was always working (the hours were awful) and Sara, who had grown her hair out to return to her natural colour—a golden blonde her clients found more reassuring—was away for two weeks every month and spent much of her time at home struggling with jet lag. They saw one another so little that they should have spent that time enjoying one another's company. Instead, their mutual jealousy grew, trapping them in an endless cycle of confrontation and reconciliation.

Cassandra was born of this tidal wave of love and violence. The little girl spent much of her childhood trying in vain to tend the wounds her parents inflicted on one another. They often apologized to her for the terrible things they said, unable to wait for her to fall asleep before they began to fight. They would sit at the foot of her bed and cry, and she would console them, embarrassed by their distress. Things only worsened as the years passed. The rise of online travel sites threatened the future of Sara's agency, which cancelled her trips and saddled her with monotonous administrative tasks to cut costs. Pax was fighting to remain relevant amid a flood of younger actors with better social networking skills. He watched, terrified, as irreverent, crowd-pleasing American series became the norm thanks to downloading and then streaming. In their respective fields, Pax and Sara both became victims of the digital revolution, which others seemed to embrace with such ease. They were only forty, but they already felt old and out of place. They were afraid, and fear is the gateway to madness. Cassandra was twelve years old when she walked in on a fight that had turned physical. Rage won out over reason that day. Her parents were gripping each other so tightly that she was afraid the veins in their arms might burst. They moved slowly, like wrestlers in the ring, their faces contorted as they threatened revenge and suffering. They were completely disconnected from the outside world, fully immersed in the nebulous network of intense emotion where crimes occur. They didn't hear or see their daughter begging them to stop, pulling on a belt, a sleeve, a collar, trying to drag them apart. A foot slipped (no one ever knew whose), sending the three of them to the floor like a single monolithic monster. When Pax and Sara stood up, Cassandra lay dizzy on the tiled floor in the kitchen, her forehead covered in blood. The physical wound wasn't serious—a dozen stitches and a scar that faded quickly—but the event marked the end of their marriage and of their family as they knew it.

It's been twelve years now, including four which looked like trench warfare; a strange, silent war during which Pax and Sara stopped all direct contact. But children are resilient, like the weeds that somehow thrive in cracks in the pavement, and Cassandra managed to grow up relatively unscathed. She quickly realized that nothing would ever bring her parents back together and she felt relieved. All she wanted was calm. Her father never spoke her mother's name again, and she learned to compartmentalize. Now Pax is like scorched earth, nourished only by an occasional summer shower, but deep down lies a layer of viscous mud left behind by recent events. An underground stream quietly irrigates the ground from below. Despite the dry, desert-like surface, life could blossom once more.

Tonight, Emi and Pax are a little drunk. They want to believe they are alike, and they manage to convince themselves they are. So many relationships are founded on misunderstandings. One of them doesn't know what love is; the other has only ever experienced the worst possible version of it. She's reserved and introverted; he's a talkative extrovert. Nevertheless, they are drawn to one another, comforted by their perception of a shared fate, though neither of them knows just how right they are. Convinced they've covered the basics (neither of them is otherwise engaged, both of them are open to the possibility of a new relationship), they discuss politics, then Emi's Japanese roots, and Pax's less exotic heritage (he was born in a small village in Champagne). He slips in a few jokes and she smiles. When the waiter explains his shift is ending and hands them the bill, Pax asks Emi to come to his place for dinner. She accepts, and he promises pasta, claiming he has a talent for Italian cuisine.

Dinner will have to wait. They kiss as soon as they walk in the door, then slide to the rug, making no effort to reach the bed or even the sofa. They undress impulsively, throwing their clothes across the room as if ridding themselves of their painful pasts—at least for an hour or two. Their bodies fit together so perfectly that they can already feel this will be more than a one-night stand. They're still naked, their limbs intertwined, satisfied and exhausted when Emi whispers, "I have to tell you about my son. I have to tell you about Alex."

A good man

". . . I was with a man, Pax Monnier, an actor who's been working with me at Demeson on a training for the employees. Didn't you get my message? I hadn't planned on getting home so late, but I'm an adult after all, aren't I? I'll be home in ten minutes . . . Yes, that's right. And I had a lovely evening, thanks for asking . . . Don't get mad, Alex, I'm tired. The fridge was full, you had everything you needed. Would you let me finish a single sentence, please? Well, if you'll believe it, Pax was recently on set with McConaughey . . . Yes, Matthew McConaughey! They get on quite well. I told him about you . . . Just the highlights, of course! You know I'd never reveal anything too personal. Have I ever? Not even once. I don't even tell your father everything . . . He was really touched. I think he's been through some difficult things himself, I can feel it. He's not like everyone else. He didn't ask any sordid questions about the details, nothing like that. He just wanted to know how you're doing. He's a good man, trust me."

Mount Olympus

After Emi leaves, Pax drags himself to his bed. His legs are weak, his breath raspy. He feels like a limp envelope, emptied of its contents—fat, bones, muscles, fluids. His thoughts are jumbled as he scratches slowly and randomly at the sheets. He wants to bang his head into a wall like he's done, or rather pretended to do, so many times on camera, but he lacks both the courage and the strength—he used all his energy to contain his panic and present a coherent front for Emi. He succeeded, but only thanks to his years of practice. He disguised his shock as fear, or maybe it was the opposite. He acted outraged, but it was sincere. He drew on the terrible feeling he'd had a year ago when he went to the police station and found out what had really happened. Since Gaspard had invited him to a party thrown by a production company after his meeting with Sveberg, he hadn't returned home until around midnight. He found a letter under his doormat asking him to get in touch with the police as soon as possible to share any information he might have about "an event" that had taken place in the building. He had immediately linked it to the noise he'd heard earlier that night. All sorts of scenarios had developed in his head, creating a dizzying flow chart of possibilities. Who was A. Winckler? If the police were investigating, it had to be serious. Had someone been wounded or even died? Was it revenge? A crime of passion? A sexual assault? A burglary gone wrong? Would they suspect him, and if they did, of what? Who else had been in the building? He'd seen a man from behind. Had he come in on a Saturday to finish some work at one of the companies located on the floors above? Or maybe he was one of those guys who distribute coupons and other flyers in all the buildings? A friend of A. Winckler? The attacker? If he admitted he'd heard worrying noises and didn't intervene, would he be charged with something? He was about to get a role that could change the future of his career. Gaspard had suggested it was as good as done. Making the front page of the tabloids might hurt his chances, tarnish his reputation. The silent dialogue with himself continued for hours, until his shame led him to rewrite the story. He went back through the situation, modifying it little by little to justify his inaction. It hadn't been that loud, anyone would have assumed it was a move, furniture being dragged around and put together, a hammer putting nails in a wall and slamming into a clumsy hand (the scream). And he'd been under pressure, his attention fully focused on his unexpected meeting with Sveberg. No, there was no way he could have known something so terrible was going on upstairs. He wasn't the kind of person who complains to their neighbours about noise in the middle of the afternoon.

In the wee hours of the morning, he convinced himself to stick to this new version of the facts. His interview at the police station that Monday was short. He told the officer he'd gone home around 4 p.m. to get a jacket and hadn't noticed anything particular. Moving things back just half an hour avoided the difficult questions entirely. As he escorted Pax out, the detective had sighed, "A nineteen-year-old kid literally beaten to a pulp and left for dead in his own flat. The world is just one big asylum . . ."

The story was already in the press, where A. Winckler was given a first name—Alex—and a face. He was a handsome boy with thick brown hair, green eyes and harmonious features, a promising science student who wasn't even remotely involved with anyone or anything dodgy. He'd moved into the furnished studio three weeks earlier to be closer to his school during exams. His parents put only enough money into his account to cover his food and school supplies. He had a mobile phone—of which there were four more recent and more desirable versions—and a mid-range laptop, but they were both found on his desk. He had many good friends, but didn't go out very much, since he was always studying, hoping to gain a place at a civilian or military flight academy. A dream now snuffed out, since the long list of his injuries included a near-total loss of vision in his right eye, which meant he would never be a pilot.

The details heightened Pax's guilt to the point that he considered confiding in someone. He needed to be reassured, to hear he had nothing to be ashamed of, that it would have been crazy to confront a monster like that, that the police would have arrived too late anyway—the experts interviewed on TV said that the attack had lasted less than ten minutes. But who could he turn to? An old saying came to mind: real friends are the ones who are willing to help you hide a body. As he went through the list of people he shared his evenings with—actors and technicians he'd met during filming, various (ex)girlfriends—his loneliness became painfully obvious. As for his family, his ex-wife hated him, his father was dead, and there was no way he could tell Cassandra. There was only his mother—a sharp-witted woman in her eighties, who would stand by him no matter what. That just about summed things up: at over fifty, he had no one but his mother to turn to. The realization was something of a blow.

Not long after he'd left the police station, Elizabeth had called him. "Have you heard about this attack? What a psycho! It happened in your neighbourhood on Saturday!"

"So?"

Elizabeth had paused, surprised by his aggressive tone. "So, nothing. I just mean you're lucky! You could have run into the guy."

Did she know something? He thought back. When he'd finished the call with Gaspard that day, he'd just told Elizabeth about the audition, not that he was going home. Plus, while Elizabeth, his agent and his daughter all knew his address, the media had never mentioned Alex's. No one knew that the crime had taken place in his building. Calm down, buddy, Pax tried to soothe himself. You're thinking like a criminal on the run. Are you a criminal? Of course not!

"The worst thing about it is that the bastard is still out there," she'd added. "If there was no motive, how do we know he won't do it again?"

This conversation added a new layer of anxiety. Up until then, Pax had only worried about the victim and the consequences of his failure to intervene. Now, he realized he could also be in danger. If the man he had glimpsed on the stairs was the attacker, he might have noticed Pax as well, and assumed he was an inconvenient witness. Damn! He became consumed by paranoia and began hugging the walls whenever he went out, checking he wasn't being followed, and jumping at the slightest noise in his building. At night, he dreamed a man in a black mask was hiding in the dark, waiting for an opportune moment to beat him up. His alarm clock generally went off just as he felt like he was dying—a death he accepted with resignation and relief. He would feel almost disappointed for a second when he woke up unharmed in his bed. He thought he was at rock bottom, but he was still on the edge of the abyss.

Everything changed the following Sunday, when two young women barely older than Alex Winckler were murdered right in front of the train station in Marseille around noon. They were just as gifted, beautiful and kind as the young man—two more names to add to the long list of victims of terrorism. Their deaths reopened unhealed wounds left by previous attacks. That same night, at a concert in Las Vegas, a man fired purposefully into the crowd, wounding and killing dozens of people and adding to the thousands of deaths from gun violence in the United States each year. Two weeks later, a dual terrorist attack in Mogadishu killed over five hundred people. Tragedies happened every day—there was no respite. The world seemed to be descending into an irreversible state of chaos as the media jumped from one event to the next, more recent, more dramatic, more profitable story.

Alex Winckler's attack faded in this volatile wave of violence. On the unspoken scale of horror, graded according to the seriousness of the attack and its geographical proximity, his case had become anecdotal. He'd survived and from a reporter's point of view, there was nothing more to say.

But how could Pax move on? Unlike the rest of the world, he thought about Alex and his attacker constantly. Wherever he looked, when he was adjusting his shirt collar in the mirror, or studying his mobile screen, the student's face was there. He began to have inexplicable sharp pains, like bites, all over his body, and he often couldn't catch his breath, so he went to see his doctor, who diagnosed panic attacks and prescribed Xanax. The drug reduced his daytime anxiety but made his nightmares so much worse that he decided to stop taking it. He lost his appetite and started smoking again. His features were drawn, and the insomnia deepened his wrinkles, making him look older. He became irritable and aggressive. Elizabeth was worried about him, but she was convinced his mental state was due to his audition with Sveberg and the wait to find out if he'd been cast. She wasn't wrong, of course, but she could never have imagined exactly how the cause and effect fitted together. She scolded him like a child, telling him to "learn to stay calm, whatever's at stake". He didn't answer. She knew nothing about what was at stake—more than his career, it was about justifying his actions and receiving absolution. Sveberg was where it had all started: the man had changed the course of fate. Without his invitation to audition on 23 September, Pax would have kept working at Thea & Co. until six o'clock. He would have arrived home after the struggle—both literal and figurative. He would have enjoyed a movie with a microwave lasagne and probably fallen asleep on his sofa. Someone would have knocked on his door later that night, and he would have been surprised to find a police officer standing there. He would have replied entirely truthfully that he hadn't heard a thing. He would have gone to bed, shocked and disturbed to learn of the attack, but with a clear conscience. Instead, he'd been waiting over a month for a decision that would finally give meaning to the whole situation.

At long last, Gaspard called.

"Hello, Pax? I've got great news, my friend. You can update your CV! Sveberg saw something in you, something dark. That's exactly what he wants for this character—a man with no illusions about human nature, you know? I felt it, too. You were different. You really impressed me!"

He'd been *different* at the Lutetia. With a single word, Gaspard had just delivered a major revelation. Pax suddenly understood what had always been missing: the fundamental drama, the struggle, the ghosts that haunt all great artists. He'd always been just another average guy with a relatively comfortable life devoid of significant obstacles. He'd never lost anyone but his father, who died peacefully in his bed at an age many people aspire to reach, and long before that, a secondary school classmate, who was not a close friend—he must have been sixteen or seventeen years old. He'd never had a serious illness and neither had anyone close to him. He'd never been raped, abused, assaulted, threatened or marginalized. He'd never wanted for anything. The worst things he'd ever experienced were his divorce and rejection at auditions.

But that 23 September had changed everything. Pax had experienced good and evil, truth and lies, bravery and cowardice. That's why Sveberg had instantly identified the irreversible and profuse distress behind Pax's mask when he walked into the Lutetia lobby that day. The director had breathed in the pheromones of anxiety and confusion. He'd taken his time to reply, but he'd made up his mind that very day. He knew instinctively what he could draw out of the actor who trembled before him, beads of sweat pearling on his neck. And his intuition turned out to be right: Pax Monnier put on a breathtaking performance during the audition that followed. His intensity surprised Gaspard, who hadn't expected such remarkable acting. This new side of Pax wasn't especially important for the film, but it opened new doors. Now the agent could put Pax's name up for ambitious projects, not only because he'd been selected by Sveberg, but because he was good—better than he'd ever been. Alex Winckler's assault had forged a new Pax Monnier, a striking actor who could move the screen itself with the sheer force of emotion he exuded. It had left behind traces of shame, fear, and excitement in him, kindling a sensitivity he had always lacked.

During the eight months before filming began, Pax did his best to find peace. He decided to leave his flat for a new place near the Porte d'Auteuil. He couldn't stand living somewhere that constantly reminded him of the assault—plus, it would make him harder to find. No one would ever be able to link Pax Monnier to Alex Winckler. The police report, like his mailbox, used his real name—Émile Moreau—which was so common that he'd had no choice but to take a pseudonym. He had chosen Monnier (his mother's maiden name), which he felt had an elegant ring to it, and Pax, long before Angelina Jolie got her hands on it. He had wanted a unique and glorious name that would be associated with him alone, whether or not he ever became a household name, but then a star who already had everything came along and stole it from him.

He rented a modest one-bedroom flat in a middle-class building filled with other renters and owners whose constant comings and goings reassured him. He kept to himself, turning the TV to a sports station as soon as he walked in. The monotone babble was company enough for him. He steered clear of the news, which always brought him back to his predicament by alluding to a crime, a brutal death, a sharp rise in violence. He drank often, but not excessively (he wasn't going to ruin everything now that his career might finally take off), hoping in vain to hold off the unwanted thoughts. He thought about the assault almost every day. He didn't fear for his own safety any more, since he'd managed to convince himself it was highly unlikely he'd ever cross paths with the attacker, but he couldn't get Alex Winckler out of his head. He kept re-watching the incident, seeing the attacker's enraged face through his eyes, feeling the desperate struggle. Then he'd wonder: was the young man disfigured or handicapped? Had he recovered? How could someone get over something so brutal? The boy was pretty much the same age as his daughter, who had never experienced such violence and wouldn't know how to deal with it. (Of course, he didn't really know this for sure, just like he didn't know what Alex Winckler really thought or felt during the attack. Pax just developed general ideas, cobbled together from details gleaned in the papers.) Time began to erode his lies, leaving him face to face with a terrible reality: he wasn't the man in a rush who thought he'd heard the sounds of someone moving in—he was a yellow-bellied, egocentric coward. He couldn't escape the suffocating feeling of guilt about his decision not to intervene and to disguise the truth.

He clung to the upcoming film like a nearly drowned survivor of a shipwreck clings to the glimmer of a faraway beach. He found some consolation in the bitterly astute character he was soon to play, seeing him as an alter ego, though the writers had considered the role so minor that they hadn't even given him a name—in the script he was just "the bartender". Pax practised his five lines so often that he occasionally slipped one in inadvertently while working with Elizabeth or having dinner with his daughter.

"You can only be betrayed by someone you love . . ."

"Dad, is something wrong?"

"Nothing's wrong, sweetheart. I was just distracted."

"That's what worries me."

Cassandra loved her father deeply, despite her distaste for the ethics lessons he regularly bestowed on her and their disagreements about her future (he'd never come around to the fact that she'd chosen to go to business school). Their unbreakable bond had been forged when she was little, and he'd carried her to school each morning perched on his shoulders. He would adjust her hat and scarf so she wouldn't get cold, check she had everything she needed, and quickly redo her hair before sending her in, then hover near the gate until a teacher shooed him away. When he wasn't filming or rehearsing, he would also pick her up at four o'clock, handing her a snack as soon as she came out. He was often the only man, surrounded by a swarm of mothers and childminders. Some of them were fans of his series and loved to have their pictures taken with him; others were disdainfully indifferent, refusing to get to know anyone who only appeared on the covers of B-list celebrity magazines.

Whenever she noticed their condescending glances, the little girl would laugh and jump up and down to distract her father, knowing instinctively how much it must hurt. She turned herself into a shield, just as she did during her parents' fights.

As an adult, she'd distanced herself a bit, but their relationship was as strong as ever. She and Pax met for dinner out once or twice a month (he didn't like having her over to his small flat, which reminded him of his mediocre success) to catch up, and they always managed to keep their dates, even when Pax began to withdraw. Cassandra was observant and she immediately noticed the change in her father. She was surprised by his intense reaction when she teased him about the Weinstein scandal and the avalanche of revelations that had shaken the industry.

"At least you don't have any skeletons in *your* closet, right? I can continue to be proud of my father?"

Pax went pale. "What exactly are you accusing me of?"

"I'm just joking, Dad. Of course I know you're not like that. Woah, chill out, or someone might think you really are guilty."

"Chill out? How do you expect me to chill out?"

"Okay, what's going on, Dad?"

Pax realized that day that he'd have to provide an explanation, or she'd hound him relentlessly. He blamed it on the film, on Sveberg's demanding nature, on the importance of it all to his career. He told her it was a major turning point for him. Filming would begin in Paris in June.

"I'm sorry, Dad. Looks like you'll have to be patient."

Well that was an understatement.

The days passed. Cassandra watched powerlessly as Pax's state of mind got worse through the autumn and winter. She suspected he was hiding something and worried about his

health, but she didn't dare broach the subject—out of respect
for his privacy and fear of finding out she was right. All she
could do was wait until the damn film was shot to see the
positive effects on her father's mood and admit she had been
wrong.

Everything went perfectly. As he stepped onto the set, Pax
felt like a League Two footballer suddenly playing on a
Premier team, listening closely for the ref's whistle should he
mess up a pass. He knew several members of the cast were
disappointed to have a lowly TV star among them and were
waiting for him to mess up. But from the first "Action!" he
outdid himself, letting go of his thoughts to achieve perfect
symbiosis with his character. Even the timbre of his voice
changed when he gravely uttered his final line: "Don't do
that." McConaughey congratulated him warmly. Peter
Sveberg gave a vague thumbs up, and a few members of the
team even applauded. His success was relative—a detail,
really, in the grand scheme of things—but for Pax, it was
huge. It was a sign he'd made, if not the right choice, then at
least a productive one on 23 September 2017. He'd just
rubbed shoulders with gods. He'd set foot on Mount
Olympus. He could have been rejected, thrown out to return
to his mortal state, but he was welcomed, acclaimed even.

When filming was over, Pax started to believe he could put
the Alex Winckler affair behind him and make peace with
himself. It would take more than a click of his fingers, but
everyone knows time heals most things. Since there was
nothing he could do to change his past, he would find a way
to overcome it. He'd learn to live with the thorn in his foot—
as most people do.

His thoughts followed the shape of a sine wave. First, he
convinced himself he hadn't done anything wrong, then he
hated himself, and then he felt ready to relinquish part of the

blame again. He began observing the behaviour of others, analysing them: the doctor who prescribed a powerful opiate to get rid of a patient who couldn't stop going on about his suffering. A bartender who kept serving drunk customers. A teacher who didn't reprimand a student out of fear of retaliation. A man who broke up with his lover via text message or worse, by ghosting her. A journalist whose opinions were for sale. People who avoided the homeless on their way home from work, but who, once comfortably ensconced on their sofas, were moved to tears by the plight of migrants. A woman who no longer visited her mother because she had Alzheimer's and wouldn't remember anyway. The young woman who refused to testify in a sexual harassment case because she feared it would jeopardize her career. The man who disappeared when he found out his girlfriend was pregnant, or who promised his mistress again and again that he'd leave his wife, or who let her go to the hospital alone for an abortion. He's watched the videos published by Swedish collective STHLM Panda hundreds of times, his eyes bulging as people in a lift with a woman being abused by her boyfriend simply look away, or as they walk past two guys urinating on a homeless man.

He thought about people living under an authoritarian regime or dictatorship, who ignore the injustice and the horrors, and sometimes even perpetuate them. About politicians who make promises on camera knowing full well they'll never be able to keep them. The list kept getting longer. He felt less lonely. All things considered, he was no worse than the next man. It was all about opportunity; the opportunity to release the monster hidden deep within each of us. Cowardice was perhaps the most common trait in the world—everyone experienced it sooner or later, one way or another, and then did their best to hide it. Pax had simply obeyed this universal rule. He'd behaved questionably, and he wasn't proud of it—at least he realized that. At least he'd given up on lying to himself.

It finally occurred to him that this long introspective journey was his penance. It would be like this until the film came out, and he simply had to accept it. *Don't* would reward his efforts and bring the Alex Winckler chapter to a close. Until then, all he could do was wait—that was how things went in the business. After filming, production continued without the actors—editing, special effects, music and more. He would just have to go home, find other ways to occupy himself, and accept that he wouldn't hear anything for weeks or months, until he got a call inviting him to the screening reserved for the team.

Thea & Co. was closed for the summer, when Elizabeth went on her annual trek through the Himalayas. Pax didn't have any other projects scheduled until November, when he was due to play a father fighting for custody of his son in an Arte miniseries (since Sveberg had hired him, he and Gaspard had agreed to choose his auditions more selectively, to further boost his reputation). He enrolled in a screenwriting workshop, a neurolinguistic programming workshop, and four lecture series at the Sorbonne. None of the seminars made much of an impression since he ended up studying the other participants in the lecture theatre, hoping to guess their darkest secrets, rather than listening to the professors. He was just killing time. By the end of August, when most people were returning home from their holidays tanned and happy, he was exhausted from running all over town.

It had been almost a year since the assault. Just one year! It felt to him like it had been a century. 23 September 2018 was a Sunday. Pax asked Cassandra to visit an art museum with him in the afternoon, then to see *As You Like It* at the Comédie-Française—a friend who worked backstage had got him three tickets. Cassandra was surprised by the day's busy schedule, and it reawakened her suspicions, but since she didn't want the theatre tickets to go to waste, she took the opportunity to introduce Pax to her girlfriend Ingrid. They'd been living together for the past six months, but Cassandra had never found the right time for them to meet, or even to tell her father she was no longer single. This was the perfect chance—the museum and the play would provide excellent topics of conversation.

Everything went to plan. Pax gave Ingrid a welcoming hug and listened attentively as she discussed Zao Wou-Ki's ink drawings and Thomas Ostermeier's stage direction. Cassandra was delighted. But the truth was that she could have introduced him to anyone that day, told him she was opening a surf school in Hawaii, or moving to a convent. Pax would have assumed the same happy expression and calm mood. His part of the conversation was completely mindless—he didn't retain any of what he heard. He was just playing a role, and boy was he good at it! Despite the nightmares it caused, he'd started taking Xanax again once the media, billboards and conversations around him began to focus on the return to school and university, bringing Alex Winckler to the fore once more.

He was thinking of Alex as the girls detailed their plans for the future—internships and then an MBA in the US. He was thinking of Alex as they discussed the music festival they planned to attend the following weekend. How was the boy now, a year after the assault? Where did he live? Was he still receiving medical treatment? Was he returning to classes? Had he begun to write an acceptable if not happy ending to the story? Pax had planned that Sunday with Cassandra and Ingrid to protect himself, but instead it fuelled his guilt.

He was still in this state of limbo—tormented by his regrets but determined to move forward and take advantage of life's opportunities—when he walked into Demeson in early October. He repeated Matthew's encouragements ("Good job, my friend. Good job!") to himself again and again, using them like a mantra to get him through the day.

He was fragile but ready when Emi Shimizu came into his life, bringing with her a subtle sense of rebirth. A few sentences, her smooth skin, fleeting smiles and magnetic presence convinced him that she was the answer to his most intimate questions. He felt like he'd been forgiven by a greater power, touched by grace and love. He wanted to cry tears of deep joy when she accepted his invitation to dinner at his place. He thought he'd been saved.

He's still shaking, huddled into a ball on his bed, an hour after Emi has left. When she said Alex's name, he jumped almost imperceptibly. For a fraction of a second, he thought: there's no way! Shimizu, Winckler . . . he had green eyes, it can't be him! Words, silence, the sound of their breath—everything was momentarily suspended in time.

Emi was brief. She cautiously told him about the disturbing violence and her son's ruined future. His state of shock and the unfathomable intensity of his pain. "I'm telling you this, Pax," she said, "because Alex is at the centre of my life, which you're now a part of as well. I'm telling you because you're friends with McConaughey and my son used to love him, so who knows . . . I'm telling you because I have nothing left to lose and the future terrifies me."

Then she cuddled up to him, her eyes closed. Her voice continued, like a light breeze across the surface of a melancholy pond. "I chose that studio because it was so quiet, isolated. I thought it would be perfect for him to study. I chose the place where he was brutally assaulted."

Pax listened in anguish, unable to organize his thoughts or utter an intelligible word.

"My son was scared and in pain while I went about my daily life. I didn't feel a thing—no twinge of the sixth sense mothers are supposed to have. Nothing at all. I only began to worry when he was late for dinner."

"It's not your fault," Pax finally managed, despite the noose he was sure he could feel tightening around his neck. "A sixth sense wouldn't have changed the outcome."

She pulled away, trying in vain to take a deep breath. "But it would have done. If he'd been taken to hospital straight away, they could have saved his eye. He might not have become the angry, depressed young man he is now. He would have had something to get up and fight for. He would have been able to make his dream a reality despite everything. He would have become a pilot! But he was alone in that empty building with no one to help him. He was alone, in a coma, in a pool of his own blood for three hours, Pax, and his mother wasn't strong enough to feel his pain."

Going mad

The world seems to swell and then shrink around Alex.

Just after the attack, there's an outpouring of sympathy. His hospital room is never empty. His mother managed to secure unpaid leave from work, followed by shorter hours. She sleeps right next to him and manages all comings and goings: family, friends, healthcare professionals from outside the hospital, police, the lawyer, the social worker, the head teacher, his maths teacher, and other people she's never heard of before, but who seem to be sincerely concerned about her son's health. His distant father—generally occupied with his new family and unsure how to proceed with his brilliant yet secretive son—also returns to the scene. He sits for hours with Alex in silence, powerless.

The young man has no memories of the assault. The space-time continuum ruptured that day, gobbling up a part of his story. He's a road cut in half by a bottomless ravine, with no bridge to cross from one side to the other—from his old life to the life that lies ahead. He remembers the long days he spent kicking a ball about in the dealership car park. He remembers the taste of peaches freshly picked with his mother at dusk, when they were still warm from the summer sun. He remembers Lune Descaux, her apathy, strange outfits and shaved head, who let him believe in love, then introduced him to heartbreak. They were only fifteen, and the young woman had suspected he was leading her on since she believed she was ugly and uninteresting. They both worked hard at making the other suffer, retaliating every time, unable to express how they really felt—the type of teenage misunderstanding that scars you for life. He remembers starting school last year, how he couldn't sleep, how he was always thinking about the final even way before his exams, how it felt like a year-long sprint. Would he reach the finish line? He remembers studying with his friends: Hugo, Baptiste, Leila and May. Despite the school's recommendation that they eat balanced meals, they stuffed themselves with kebabs, pizzas, burgers and chips. It was their only real break, their outlet to relieve the pressure of responsibility and sacrifice. For just an hour, they went back to being who they really were—a gang of teenagers hungry for life and freedom. He remembers his plan to become a pilot. That dream was born the day his grandmother sat him down in front of her on her CB750 and revved the engine. He must have been seven. He remembers how excited he was when the motorbike lurched forward, air filling his throat as his stomach rose up into his chest. When he felt the intoxicating euphoria, he immediately knew he wanted more. He wanted to take off, to fly, to break the sound barrier, to toy with the boundaries between earth and sky—and that feeling never left him. It guided him through every turn in his schooling, driving him as he memorized pages of chemical formulas (he loved physics, but hated chemistry). He remembers the ordered, even benevolent world he used to live in, where his efforts were always rewarded. He was one of the best students in his class, but he remained modest and relaxed. He was often funny, and always happy to help others, despite the bitter competitiveness all around him. He was well liked by everyone. He was happy and fulfilled, even after his parents' divorce. Luckily, they'd been mostly honest with one another, and always with him.

He remembers his past as if it were a play or a choreographed dance. He remembers everyone's parts, including his own, but watches from the audience, removed from the show upon which the theatre will soon collapse. 23 September 2017, between 4 and 5 p.m.

When he wakes up, his parents, doctors and visitors awkwardly tell him what happened. The brutality of the attack could be measured by his resulting injuries and disability. He had lost 90 per cent of his vision in his right eye. Their words plunge him into a suffocating, opaque, frozen sea. His now dark iris leaves him with mismatched eyes, which he gouges out in his nightmares. He understands that he lives on the other side of the ravine now—a scorched continent where the horizon is just a trembling line moving further and further away. He's dead, but he seems to be the only one who knows it. Everyone around him shoulders their share of the lie and does their best to convince him that "everything will be okay", and that "it'll just take some time". Technology is evolving so quickly! Pretty soon, AI will replace his eye and he'll go back to living "a normal life"!

Shedding the skin of the whole and happy boy he once was, a new Alex wriggles free, terrified, angry, and full of despair. He's constantly looking for clues, for any sort of explanation. He's obsessed with a single question that turns round and round in his head like an unbearable refrain: why me, why me, why me? Did he do something—a look, a word—to provoke his tragedy? He has a flash and suddenly remembers going out to buy something. But what? Where? What time? The rest is a black hole. Empty. No images, no sounds, no feelings, no witnesses. The only thing the police know for sure is that the attacker used brass knuckles. There was no blood or hair under his nails or on his clothes, no unidentified DNA in the flat. Maybe they'd find something if they looked harder, but Alex is alive, and the forensic teams have been summoned to handle more dramatic cases.

He feels like he's going mad. Whenever he's alone in his room, he bangs his head against the wall to make sure he's not dreaming, adding new bruises to his black-and-blue body. The facts defy all reasoning. He considers even the most extreme possibilities—he was drugged, he's the subject of a secret experiment, he's living in an alternate reality—but finally has to admit he's probably just a random victim of senseless violence. He's gobsmacked by the realization that he was wrong about everything. The world is primitive, uncivilized, hostile, unfair and unpredictable. A person's efforts and good character offer no protection—or perhaps he's been wrong about his own merits, and he deserved what happened. His world begins to crack, then it falls to pieces. Rage fills him, overwhelms him, and a torrent of toxic lava scorches his beliefs and convictions along with the joy and trust he used to feel, leaving behind nothing but a blackened heart, aged before its time. He refuses the gifts that are supposed to ease his suffering (chocolates, books and CDs), handing them out to the healthcare assistants instead. He throws the Brazilian amulet from his father's new wife in the bin. He stops opening the new letters and emails he receives daily (his mother used to read some of them, but the same trite expressions kept appearing: "I can't begin to imagine what you're feeling", "we're with you in thought", "what a terrible crime", etc.). He doubts his friends' sincerity, begins to suspect they're motivated by morbid curiosity or some sort of selfish superstition, as if hurrying to his bedside might ward off any danger on their own paths. He's not entirely wrong: everyone suddenly felt very vulnerable when they learned that Alex—the good friend and perfect son—had been assaulted. Seeing him lying there with IVs in his arm reassures them—lightning never strikes twice in one place. One person's misfortune guarantees the safety of those around him. They lean over his bed, studying their friend, troubled by his changed appearance: his dishevelled hair, his pale skin, his vacant gaze. They can tell he's not there, but they can't find the words to describe his absence. Alex is in orbit around a planet he no longer recognizes and wants no part of.

As soon as he's regained some of his strength, he asks for the visits to stop. His mother complies, keeping people away. Emi Shimizu knows what the imperious need for solitude looks like. She makes her child's pain her own and accepts his darkness, hoping it will be temporary. When she kisses his forehead and strokes his hand, he doesn't pull away, and that's enough for her. The flow of people quickly slows, then disappears altogether. His loved ones have gone back to their simple lives. They've done their duty, shown their support. What else can they do? It's autumn now, and the news, with the seasonal rise in violence and several terrorist attacks, gives them perspective on Alex's misfortune and helps them overcome their guilt. The show must go on. Hugo, Baptiste, Leila and May return to the library, bury themselves in their work. Alex's father also stops visiting so frequently—since it's what Alex wants. He hoped to strengthen his bond with his son, reclaim the place in Alex's life that he'd left empty for so many years, but it didn't work. After weeks of silence, he tried to have a conversation with his son, but he was clumsy. He talked about his upcoming holidays, his wife's pregnancy, the house they were looking to buy in the country, the tennis court they would build there. "I'll teach you. I won tons of tournaments at your age." Alex simply turned away to highlight the absurdity of his father's comments and put an end to the exchange.

Christophe takes offence at this. He refuses to let his own son push him away, even though he was entirely responsible for their distant relationship. Insulted, he goes after Emi, criticizing her for turning their son into an "academic machine" and implicitly blaming her for the assault. After all, he hadn't wanted to rent that studio. He'd told her that with a workload like Alex's, it was better to have someone else handle quotidian things like food and laundry. Of course, the real reason was because it was inconvenient for him—he had other projects to fund, like the birth of his second child and the beautiful country house he'd been eyeing since the spring (he was playing the long game to get the best price). But now he claims he knew, that he could feel it, that Emi should have listened to him because *he* had the sixth sense she lacked. It wounds her deeply. But Emi doesn't need her ex-husband's insinuations to deem herself an unfit mother. When she found Alex on the floor that day, she knew she would never forgive herself. She doesn't defend herself to Christophe. In an empty voice, she tells him he's right—it's all her fault. He realizes he's gone too far, that he's kicked her when she was already down, but it's too late. Now this terrible accusation will always fill the space between them.

After that, Emi and Christophe only communicate via brief text messages. They're careful never to bump into one another at their son's bedside. Six months after the assault, Alex is transferred to a rehabilitation centre. He's the youngest patient there, and the nurses, doctors and physiotherapists make his recovery their personal mission. The boy has to get better—if he doesn't, their whole world might collapse, too. Their investment pays off. Alex makes great progress. He begins walking down the corridors, his limp slowly improving until it becomes almost imperceptible. His mismatched eyes, fragile frame and shoulder-length brown hair (he refuses to cut it) give him a fascinating, unreal appearance— as if he's just stepped out of a manga. But whenever he finds himself in front of a mirror, all he sees is a ruin. He clenches his fists and waits for the lights to go out and the noise to quiet before giving in to the sobs. He feels tiny beside a wall that reaches up to the sky. I'm nineteen years old and my life is over, he thinks. I'm fucking blind in one eye, he thinks as he cries. He imagines his friends concentrating on their work or having fun playing video games, and he thinks: why me, why me, why me? He overturns the table, kicks the wall. He's a child lost in a crowd of adults. Then he suddenly thinks: why *not* me? His mind wanders, weakens; he wants it to end, wants to be dead for real.

Emi felt it before anyone else. She was unable to prevent the assault, but in this hospital, she can predict a rise in his temperature or that he'll regain feeling in a limb. She can interpret a tremor, fluttering eyelids, slowed breathing. She convinces the psychiatrist to prescribe something for Alex and is allowed to extend her visiting hours. At night, she massages her son with a homemade blend of hemlock and sweet almond oil until he falls asleep. She nods off next to him, exhausted, but wakes ten times a night to whisper, "Please hold on. Please fight, sweetheart." If he dies, she has sworn—without a hint of melodrama—that she'll die with him. "Hold on, Alex." His condition stabilizes, and the medication begins to improve his mood. His bones heal. His face has changed, but it's still beautiful—his skin has smoothed out, erasing almost all traces of the attack. The concussion hasn't affected his reasoning abilities or sensory processing. His joints and muscles sometimes cause him unbearable pain, but the vertigo, migraines and difficulties speaking are gone. He still has a hard time judging distances and size, so he bumps into things and stumbles often, but he get around well enough for daily life. The team of healthcare professionals all agree that he can finish his rehabilitation at home with his mother. It's a November morning, and Alex is reminded of a Baudelaire poem: *When the cold heavy sky weighs like a lid / On spirits whom eternal boredom grips / And the wide ring of the horizon's hid / In daytime darker than the night's eclipse.* He slowly dresses in the clothes his mother has brought, stops, starts again, his chest tight. Does he really have to leave this limbo and return to a world that is no longer his? *When the world seems a dungeon, damp and small, /Where hope flies like a bat, in circles reeling, / Beating his timid wings against the wall / And dashing out his brains against the ceiling.* "Come on," urges Emi. "The taxi's waiting. I'm right here; I'll always be here for you. You know that, right?"

Before going to pick him up from the rehabilitation centre, she made sure to fill the kitchen cupboards and the fridge with his favourite foods: honey Cheerios, chocolate bars, yogurts, freshly squeezed orange juice. Sonia and Izuru called to tell her how happy they were that "the worst is behind him now, right?"

The naive joy in their voices was comforting, but now that she's watching her son as he hesitates to step outside, as he climbs into the taxi like a man on his way to his execution, she knows it's far from over. Alex glues his face to the car window, silently watching the road, struggling to process the swirling images. *When trawling rains have made their steel-grey fibres / Look like the grilles of some tremendous jail, /And a whole nation of disgusting spiders / Over our brains their dusty cobwebs trail.* He tries in vain to thwart the growing terror as the car nears its destination. As the door to the back seat opens, fear pounces like a voracious animal who's been lying in wait. It tackles him, overtakes him, devours him. Pure, uncontrollable fear which whispers in his ear that the psycho will come back. Maybe he's already here, hiding in the lift, ready to finish the job. Alex rips the keys from his mother's hand, then runs with his limp up the stairs and into the flat. "Jesus, hurry up, Mum. What the hell are you waiting for!" he shouts at her. *Suddenly bells are fiercely clanged about /And hurl a fearsome howl into the sky / Like spirits from their country hunted out /Who've nothing else to do but shriek and cry.* He slams the door shut behind her and locks it. He's drenched in sweat, and his stomach and head hurt. The nauseating smell of blood comes back to him, the blow before the coma. He clings to the details around him though he knows them by heart, hoping to calm his thoughts. The chest of eight drawers in the hallway, the decorative ceramic dish on top shaped like a maple leaf, the understated light fittings, the laminate flooring, the bouquet of dried flowers, the incense burner. Emi is flustered. She didn't expect this. She thought he would be okay here, a place associated with happy memories from his years at secondary school. She saw it as a peaceful retreat where he would feel safe. Now she realizes that nothing can reassure Alex, because no one knows who attacked him, or why, or even how it happened. When something happens for no reason, it can happen again, at any time. Her son now looks like an emaciated stray cat, his one good eye feverishly scanning the room, constantly on the lookout for imminent danger. She would like to take him in her arms and envelop him with love, but she can't reach him—he's not really there. She swears that nothing bad will ever happen to him again. The ironic laugh her promise elicits feels like a knife to the heart. And the next day, as she's about to leave for work, he won't let her go. He clutches desperately at her coat until she gives in and collapses onto the floor with him. *Then long processions without fifes or drums /Wind slowly through my soul. Hope, weeping, bows / To conquest. And atrocious Anguish comes / To plant his black flag on my drooping brows.*

For Alex, Emi agrees to have their front door reinforced and to purchase a new mobile phone for which he alone will have the number, to ensure he can always reach her. She buys a taser, which emits a 5,000-volt jolt (she read the description three times, horrified by its destructive power), for him to keep on his belt, as well as five canisters of pepper spray, which he places in the kitchen, the bathroom, the loo, the hallway, and the lounge. He spends the first few days holed up in his room, carefully studying the sounds coming from outside. Then he moves on to the opposite strategy, placing headphones over his ears and turning them all the way up with his eyes closed, as if daring death to take him by surprise. He refuses to leave the flat, except for his therapy appointments (he has no choice), but even then, it's a carefully planned ritual. Emi turns on the alarm, places one of the pepper sprays in her handbag, and leads the way to the lift as Alex follows close behind. They walk together to the train station (the psychiatrist's office is in Paris), wait for the train with their backs against a billboard, then sit in the seats next to the conductor's car. When they reach the city, Alex stands to the left of his mother, carefully placing her in his blind spot, but he still demands constant reassurance, afraid he's seen suspicious movements on her side. People turn and stare when they feel the tangible tension coming off the strange pair. Unbeknownst to them, their judgemental glances are like darts in the back of Alex's neck and spears in Emi's stomach.

Alex never says anything about his sessions. Emi hopes the psychiatrist will manage to repair the damage that's been done. She told him that her son has turned their flat into a fortress and has a growing number of OCD tendencies, but she was unable to find the right words to say what she really feels: that her son exists outside what people commonly accept as reality. He rejects the past, the present and the future as he floats in his room as though in an isolation chamber, using music (he spends hours composing songs on his computer) as his only refuge. He cycles through alternate phases of anger and despondency with his mother, blaming her for everything—she talks too loudly or not enough, she was supposed to get AA not AAA batteries, she didn't choose the right time for physiotherapy, the coffee's bitter, she comes home late—then apologizing as he holds back tears and goes to run her a bath or boil water for her tea. Emi never complains. She's holding on, though God knows how. She confides in Langlois, who recommends she should avoid expecting anything from Alex any time soon. She shouldn't push him—the academic year is down the drain, and he doesn't know what comes next. His one-eyed vision has slowed him down considerably. Langlois encourages her to break their routine and try to cultivate a wide range of sensory experiences, so she manages to make new dinners each night from colourful ingredients she hurriedly purchases during her lunch break. In the evening, she talks to her son about the beech trees losing their leaves in the breeze, the sound of the wind gusting through the apartment buildings, the white frost on the ferns, the first snow melting in the winter sun. She also passes on messages from his friends, but she doesn't urge him to call them back.

One day in mid-December, she leaves the apartment for an entire Sunday, so Christophe can spend some time with Alex. It's also the first break she's allowed herself in three months. She spends five hours walking in the forest in her hiking boots and a comfortable fleece, filling her lungs with oxygen, enjoying the presence of the trees and the thick carpet of rotting leaves beneath which life continues to teem. When she returns home, worn out but restored, she learns that Christophe left after twenty minutes, annoyed by his son's insolent silence, but she doesn't utter a single criticism.

On Christmas Day, she organizes a small dinner with Sonia and Izuru—no tree or decorations. As he steps into the flat, her father is holding a beige canvas bag, from which he pulls a shogi board. Emi's heart jumps as she recognizes the varnished wood polished by her grandfather's fingers in the garden in Takeno. She can see his spider-like hands with their prominent veins and soft skin, which led her to the top of the hill when she was eight years old, to the place where she built her invisible defences. Alex sits down at the game, slides the pieces around one by one, listens as Izuru explains what each one represents—the king, the gold general, the silver general, the lance, and the knight—and his unexpected curiosity fills his mother with hope.

Langlois warns Emi. Though he's never met Alex, he knows it will take much longer than a few months for him to recover and begin to enjoy life again. Though it's difficult to accept, time moves at a different pace for Alex. Those who have never had a near-death experience know nothing of the fear it sparks, so they tend to set deadlines. When people talk about Alex, they say things like: "he's young", "at that age it's easy to get back on your feet again", "he needs to turn the page", "it's just a question of willpower". Alex doesn't have any willpower any more. Fear and disillusionment have destroyed everything. Nevertheless, he occasionally thinks he would like to cross the abyss and return to the world he used to live in. But how? His attacker ripped him away and relegated him to this parallel universe, where he wanders aimlessly, an empty shell with nowhere to go. He tries every now and again to be truly present. He takes off his headphones, opens his window and listens to the children playing in the nearby park, but it always leaves him feeling breathless, like a fish out of its bowl. Sometimes he goes into his mother's room, to use the only mirror in the flat (at his request, Emi removed the one in the bathroom so he wouldn't have to see himself—his gaunt features and dead eye), but his reflection sends him into a panic every time. Everything around him reminds him of what happened: new operations in February; the exam period, which runs through to July; matriculation dates for flight academies; application dates for government jobs (he has no intention of applying, but he couldn't even if he wanted to—he's been off the grid for too long); the World Cup, which he had planned to watch and celebrate with his friends, certain that France would win the year he turned twenty. He was right: France earns its second star, but he doesn't celebrate anything at all—neither the victory nor his birthday. The holiday home they've rented for the summer has a tennis court, which he can see from the bedroom where he's locked himself away. It reminds him of the list of "strongly discouraged" activities his ophthalmologist gave him, to preserve his remaining eye, which includes anything involving balls and—to rub salt in the wound—martial arts. He can't even learn to defend himself. And even if he were allowed, would he be able to? Sometimes his chronic pain flares up terribly, turning him into an old man in a twenty-year-old body that's addicted to morphine and constantly mumbling: why me, why me, why me?

September rolling round again is the worst part. A whole year already! Anniversaries always seem to push people to evaluate the past and assess their chances for the future, and reality smacks Alex in the face. He contemplates what he is and what he could have been, and he has a revelation: he's empty, absent, hollow. As far back as he can remember, he followed a path designed to take him somewhere he can never go now. What's left without his plans? He worked hard to get the best grades. He was a good student, a good son, a good friend; a good soldier, as the saying goes. He did what was expected of him, upheld his end of the bargain, but he should have read the small print: there's nothing to replace the rug that's been pulled out from under him.

On 23 September 2018, as Hugo, Baptiste, Leila and May head to the cinema together, and as Christophe and Pauline order a new cot, and the world keeps spinning as if nothing has changed, Alex Winckler hides under his desk, his knees pulled tight to his chest, chanting Radiohead lyrics he feels were written just for him: *This isn't happening, I'm not here, I'm not here, in a little while, I'll be gone.* But when he wakes up at dawn the next morning, his limbs still asleep, he finds his mother sitting motionless in the corridor with her chin resting on her shoulder, her eyes darting frantically to and fro beneath her lids, and her hands clutched together so tightly that the tips of her fingers have gone white. He remembers why he has to keep living. He picks her up, wrapping his arms around her waist and struggling to keep her from falling. He drags her as best he can to her room and puts her down on the bed, then unbuttons her shirt, which seems to be constricting her breathing. Emi's hair is loose and wild, and a strand falls into her open mouth. Alex gently removes it, then hurries to the bathroom for a damp flannel for her forehead. He leans down and whispers, *Mum, Mum, Mum.*

This isn't the first time he's found his mother in such a state. They don't talk about it, don't even allude to it. It's a mystery that has recently come to fill the space between them. Is she ill? Exhausted? Sleepwalking? After each incident, Emi comes out in the morning as if nothing has happened. Her face is glowing and she's dressed and coiffed to perfection as usual. She kisses her son's forehead and smiles. "See you tonight!" she says cheerily. He watches as she walks to the station, her thin, graceful frame slowing as she nears a cluster of laurel trees. She removes a leaf and slips it into her pocket. Who would ever guess that a shadow is slowly growing inside her?

Filled with love, he vows to protect her, whatever the cost. So when his mother mentions that man again, and suggests inviting him over—to the flat where no one but his grandparents, his father, and a handful of healthcare professionals have been for the past fourteen months—Alex accepts, hoping Pax will be part of the solution.

Who's holding the gun?

It's a trap, thinks Pax. A trap I set for myself with no way out.

Emi suggested he come over one Sunday. He claimed he had plans for the next few weekends. That gave him time to solve the equation, to study his options. The easiest thing would be to put an end to their relationship. He knows how to break up with women, how to make himself the bad guy without lying. He simply tells them he's a sucker for beauty, but that he has no intention of committing. It's better for him to leave before hurting them, since they've done nothing to deserve that. But this time, things aren't so easy—he's in love. Three weeks of passionate dates have made it clear how he feels about Emi. If he'd known who she was, he would have put up walls, of course. But would they have held? As soon as he sets eyes on Emi his heart starts racing, he loses track of his thoughts, and all willpower melts away. Jesus, why? Why did he have to cross paths with this woman, or rather, with her son? Is it pure chance? Or divine punishment? Karma? He remembers the strange intuition he felt last year when Sveberg invited him to audition. Pax was the bullet in the barrel, ready to ricochet from one body to another. The shot's been fired. But who's holding the gun?

It's early. They met at Demeson before heading together to the training venue. He's sweating and can't catch his breath and she's worried, afraid he might pass out. She offers to call a doctor, suggests he needs to be properly checked out since it could be a heart attack, but he refuses, swears that despite appearances everything is fine. She insists. He says she just doesn't understand. She thinks she has an idea: her request has made him uncomfortable. Meeting a traumatized young man who's consumed by anger probably isn't anyone's idea of fun. She places her hand on Pax's and apologizes for pressuring him. He's fallen to pieces. He can no longer suppress his guilt by toying with different interpretations—he could have saved Alex's eye, and he didn't. That's all there is to it. He despises himself and is about to confess. But then he stops: he can no longer ignore the consequences of his actions. A confession would ease his conscience, but it wouldn't heal Alex and it would destroy Emi. Their unexpected bond is keeping her afloat, that much is clear. Her features soften when she's in his arms. He's the source of her energy, just as she is his. This is what makes the situation so dizzying. Pax doesn't dare imagine how she would feel if she learned the truth. Disgusted, most likely, with him, but even more so with herself. He refuses to put her through that—Emi already has plenty of monsters to hate. He resigns himself to the idea that he must keep quiet. But how will he enforce his own silence? Will he be able to live with the secret? Can he lock it away in some far corner of his soul and throw away the key? Never think of it again? Will he be able to look the woman he loves (and her son) in the eye? Will he be able to lie day after day without ever crumbling? To protect her, he must betray her. That's the crux of it.

He watches her as she leans over her desk, alphabetizing the files she'll hand out to the participants after the session. There are only two left before the end of the training. She's wearing her white blouse and straight, pale grey skirt which enhance her beauty, making her radiant, when on anyone else the outfit would be bland and unfashionable. She focuses on her work. Each of her movements is precise and efficient. Pax pours himself a cup of coffee and holds one out to her. He shifts his weight from one foot to the other and back again, lost in his thoughts, until a yelp pulls his wandering mind back. She's dropped her cup. The coffee has stained her shirt and spread to her skirt. It drips slowly onto the floor, creating a dark puddle beneath her chair. She glances at Pax in despair and hurries to the toilets to clean her clothes—the taxi is already waiting downstairs to take them to the training centre, where the session is set to begin in less than an hour. When she comes back, the stain is still visible on her chest. She runs her thumb over the fabric, noticing the roughness created by all the rubbing, and focuses on this sensation as she fends off the emotions assailing her. She purses her pale lips and puts on her blazer and scarf.

"It's no big deal," says Pax. "It'll disappear eventually."

"I don't think so," whispers Emi. "Some stains are permanent."

They both go quiet, each of them besieged by their own thoughts. Pax is a lab rat locked in a maze, on a quest for a reward and terrified of punishment. And Emi has just read the name Jérôme Tellier (Christian P.'s workmate) on the list of today's participants. Tellier! But the doctor had signed him off on long-term leave, along with the third employee who had been in the lorry that day—a temp worker on his first day at Demeson. The temp had a sprained hip and Tellier had broken his collarbone and his leg—they were incredibly lucky, given Christian P.'s injuries. While the temp had disappeared from Demeson's files before Emi could even put a face to the name, she remembers the friendship between Christian P. and Jérôme Tellier all too clearly. During the investigation, their bond served as an argument for accidental death over suicide: how could Christian P. have voluntarily risked the life of a man he'd worked with and been close friends with for twenty years? Every summer, their families rented a house in Brittany together, where they had barbecues and played ping-pong and boules in the garden, then volleyball and football on the beach with their children.

Suicide was inconceivable for Jérôme Tellier and Christian P.'s wife. They would have had to concede that they'd cherished a murderer, a heartless madman with no morals. They would have had to admit that their lives had meant nothing to him. Christian P. had a strong personality and always got his way, but he never, they said, again and again, never would have harmed his loved ones! Nevertheless, Jérôme Tellier had had doubts since he'd woken up on a stretcher in an ambulance. He knew Christian P. had been deeply wounded by HR's final offer to help him "transition to a new career", and Jérôme had mentioned this to Emi not long before the accident—a day when they just happened to find themselves sitting together in the canteen. The end of August was particularly busy, and Christian P. (who generally no longer handled straightforward personal moves) had been asked to "wear the collar" again. That's the expression he'd used one evening as he drank a pastis with his friend, exhausted from lifting, carrying, setting down and climbing for hours in the hot sun. "The collar is tight and the lead is short, but the dog is mean, and far from dumb. He'll bite his masters before he kicks the bucket," he'd added. Christian P. had changed over the previous few weeks. He'd gained weight around the middle and lost what little hair he'd had left. He'd been stressed out and belligerent, when he was usually so eventempered and accommodating. That's why Jérôme Tellier had warned Emi Shimizu, between a yogurt and some overripe grapes, that he was worried.

"Yes, I see," Emi had replied. "Have him send me an email. I'll be happy to meet with him."

Tellier was disappointed. He had hoped she'd take the initiative. Instead, he was supposed to ask Christian P. to write to the company's health and safety manager, and he already knew exactly what his friend would say: *I'm not the problem! THEY'RE the problem!* So the conversation ended there. He wouldn't have known how to change Christian P.'s mind.

Emi usually uses the taxi ride to go over the upcoming training with Pax. Today, she keeps quiet, drafting an email to the HR manager, who failed to let her know Jérôme Tellier was back, though in an administrative position, and that he'd be at the training session. It's probably since her office is at the other end of the corridor—and because she has limited power. She's getting her anger out, but she knows she'll never actually send it. She'd have to explain why Tellier is so important, why she needed time to prepare to see him again, why her throat is so tight. But she can't. She won't ever say anything to anyone.

When they reach the venue, she lets Pax pay the driver and hurries into the room. She quickly waves hello to the participants, looks for her name card, then sits down and focuses all her attention on her notes. She places her handbag on her lap, hoping it will hide her stained blouse. The second actor Elizabeth hired for the scenes is already on stage setting up. He's a young man who's just graduated from drama school. His laid-back attitude and extreme confidence seem to announce that he won't be doing this for long, that he'll soon be signing autographs rather than participants' attendance slips. He paces the stage and clears his throat, trying in vain to catch Emi's eye. Pax can see what's going on, and for good reason: the boy is him twenty or thirty years earlier—a handsomer version. He remembers practising his charms on women, so full of his youthful self, so convinced he was free, invincible and fearless. This Thomas (that's his name) reminds Pax of his own eternal quest, and for a millisecond, those demons reappear—the imperious need to succeed, to earn the audience's approval and recognition. He's nearly blindsided by the chilling thought that an army of young talent is waiting in the wings to steal his rewards. He's jealous twice over. Both of any interest Emi might show (none for the moment), and of the top billing the kid might steal from him (even though they'd never be in direct competition). This day is becoming truly suffocating. Pax steps out into the corridor for a few moments, thinks of Sveberg, of *Don't*, which will restore some balance to his life—but when? He keeps coming back to Emi Shimizu and Alex Winckler, to the trap. They spin round and round in his mind as he fills a cup with water, dips his fingers in it and wets his forehead to find his way back to a sense of reason and calm.

When he re-enters the full auditorium, filled with the easy laughter of the employees who are pleased to be spending their half-day watching a skit rather than breaking their backs climbing in and out of removal lorries, he immediately notices Emi has gone. Her seat is empty. There's no handbag, pen, tablet or scarf on her seat. She's left without telling him.

"She didn't feel well," explains Thomas. "Thought she was coming down with something. She said you'd be able to handle things on your own."

Pax smiles, disoriented. Everything suddenly seems to be slipping through his fingers. Two hours ago, Emi Shimizu's tender lips kissed his, exerting their magnetic power on his heart. She was worried about him, even offered to postpone introducing him to Alex. Then she spilled her coffee, and it was as though the stain had ruined more than a piece of fabric. Now she's left without a word. What does this mean?

"No problem, we don't need her," he replies.

He climbs onto the stage and opens with a joke. The

audience applauds rowdily, but all he can hear or feel is a series of dizzying slaps to the face. Thomas jumps in, keeping their focus, as Pax stares at Emi's empty seat.

At around 12.30 p.m., when the session's over, he finds a message on his phone from Gaspard letting him know that Sveberg intends to film a few more scenes with McConaughey. Which means the screening won't be any time soon. Is his career coming down with something, too? He's not even surprised. It's just further proof of the thread woven by the Fates that runs from Emi Shimizu to Matthew McConaughey via Alex Winckler, to him. He decides then and there that he'll meet Alex. He's ready now. He'll confront his remorse, take charge of his shame, and do his best to behave in a dignified fashion, by giving the boy—from whom he's taken so much—what he can. Maybe then he'll be able to find his way out of this maze.

Cloud of cotton

When she gets off the train, Emi goes for a walk in the frozen woods. The wind is invigorating, despite the stinging rain. She doesn't shield herself from it. She gathers a bouquet of brown-and-gold leaves, studies their varied shades, tries to forget herself in them, but it's not enough—it's never enough any more.

Earlier, as people were taking their seats at the training centre, Jérôme Tellier tapped her on the shoulder, forcing her to look up from her papers. His deeply wrinkled face bore the marks of sleepless nights, of constantly dwelling on the same question, the same memories.

"I'm sorry to bother you, Ms Shimizu, but I was wondering if you'd received the report from the investigation. Did they find anything new?"

"They concluded it was an accident," replied Emi, hardly able to breathe. "A terrible accident. I'm pleased to see you're doing better."

Tellier sighed. "Thank you. It's good that you're implementing these additional procedures. We must have missed something."

Now, Emi's pale hand lets go of the leaves, except for the largest, whose stem she rolls carefully between her fingers like a talisman. Tellier's last words echo in her mind. Did he choose them purposely? She'd been almost certain he would want more information, but he went back to his seat without asking if Christian P. had got in touch with Emi before the accident or if she had any personal feelings about the incident. What would she have said if he'd asked?

Emi found the email from Christian P. about two weeks after his funeral, in mid-September. He had sent it two days before the accident, late in the evening of 29 August. It had been buried amid dozens of other emails in her secondary inbox—her main inbox was reserved for messages sent by company executives. It was the end of the summer and everyone was talking about the return to work and school, leaving Emi in deep despair. Alex refused all her suggestions for distance learning and stayed locked in his room with the shutters closed. Everywhere she looked—billboards, newspapers, shops filled with groups of eager young people—she was confronted with joyful excitement about the first days of school. The contrast between the anticipatory buzz that filled the city and the silence of her apartment, where the person she loved most in the world was wasting away, was hard to deal with. To make matters worse, the psychiatrist had recently warned her that Alex's anxiety and depression weren't improving despite his therapy sessions, and that he'd need a stronger course of medication. For the first time since her son's assault, she felt as though she couldn't cope; as though she too would fall apart. When dealt a bad hand, people put up defences around themselves—some of which are stronger than others. Emi Shimizu had built an invisible levee into which events crashed in vain while she watched, impassively, from a distance. She was present but absent, managing the basics, hiding behind the mask of her aloof beauty. Information washed over her without her absorbing any of it—that's what had happened with Jérôme Tellier's concerns. She'd heard them, then forgotten them. But Christian P.'s accident had been a terrible tidal wave, which brought with it a body. The ensuing shock forced her to wake up, only to find her eyes brimming with tears and the corridors closing in as her life became a succession of press releases, announcements, medical examiner reports full of terrifying terms, and forms to fill out.

It was on a hunt for one of these administrative documents that she found Christian P.'s email. The subject heading was "In case you're interested". Four pages without a single spelling mistake or typo. In it, the man told of everything he'd done for the company. He'd never counted his overtime, was incredibly competent and selfless, and loved a job well done. In return, the company had served him up a steady dose of lies, humiliation and hostility. They had pushed him, he wrote, not to the bottom of the ladder, but off it entirely. They offered to train him as a metalworker, roofer or blacksmith! At his age, with his neck and lower-back injuries! Really they were offering him a path that led to an internship and then to unemployment—a direct route to poverty and dependence on the state! The company had sucked him dry, and now that he might need something from them, since he wasn't fit to begin a new life doing back-breaking work for someone else, now that he was worn out, tired and empty, they were kicking him out, all the while pretending it was because he was over-qualified, like getting rid of a spouse you no longer love by telling them they're too good for you. During the merger, added Christian P., Demeson's CEO, like an emperor addressing the people, had given a speech littered with opportunistic allusions to football which focused on the "shared adventure" at the company and the "common good". To conclude, he had quoted Alexandre Dumas: "One for all, and all for one."

It was all lies. No one was there for him now. The employees should have come together to protest, to demand the company take care of the people who had contributed to its prosperity, the way children should take care of their elderly parents, but they'd been too afraid. "So, Ms Shimizu," wrote

Christian P., "I still have free will. It's the only thing I have left. I refuse your pity, lies and fraud. If the company wants to see me go, to erase my name and my thirty years of loyal service, then I'll go. But believe me, you won't be forgetting me any time soon."

When she'd finished reading, she sat motionless at her screen for the rest of the day. A few people came into her office, and she answered their questions. She was present, but absent. Little by little, the corridors emptied. The September sunlight shone on the bare walls, heightening her loneliness. That last sentence burned into her mind: *you won't be forgetting me any time soon.* It had broken through her defences, letting in a flood of questions. She wanted to be eight years old again and seek refuge on the hill that overlooked Takeno. She closed her eyes and held tight to her grandfather's hand to stop the wave dragging her down. She almost deleted the email, but decided in the end to archive it in a file with a neutral name. She went home, where Alex was waiting for her, realizing she would now have to live not only with her son but also with Christian P. She would always be painfully aware of her limits, of her powerlessness and her failings; her doubts would always plague her. She felt herself going under. She went to bed early but couldn't fall asleep. At 3 a.m., exhausted, she suddenly realized relief was within her grasp. She had never taken any drugs, and very few prescription medicines, but she'd read enough books and seen enough films to know how morphine worked. She had even worried when the doctor had prescribed it for Alex. He'd reassured her that in his case, as long as they kept to the recommended dosage, the drug would relieve his pain and no more. "It's true," he'd added, "some idiots enjoy opening the capsules to crush the beads and snort them, but what can we do about it? We can't always be watching." Since Alex's pain levels varied, and he needed to be able to manage unpredictable flare-ups, the prescription was for much more than he usually needed. So, by following advice found on specialist forums, Emi Shimizu learned to surf the wave and keep the turmoil at bay. Over the past two months, morphine has become her ally, her lifeline.

Alex is surprised to see her home so soon. She claims there's renovation work being done at the office, so she'd rather work from home. He knows she's lying. From living cloistered as they do, they've learned to notice the slightest variations in each other's moods. He suggests they have tea together. She's touched—it's a major effort for him to sit down in the kitchen in the middle of the afternoon. They drink in silence. She tries to concentrate on the physical sensations: the hot water on her lips, in her throat, burning her oesophagus. She thinks of the cloud of cotton she'll dive into later, where her anxiety will be erased like chalk from a blackboard. She thinks of the autumn colours.

"Mum. Mum!"

She jumps.

"Someone rang the doorbell."

She gets up to open the door, and Alex disappears into his room with his cup. There's no one there. The delivery man has gone, but there's a bouquet of white camellias on her mat. The card reads: *See you Sunday if you'll still have me. Pax.*

CB750

They stand opposite each other like two marble statues. Pax chose a black leather jacket and a pair of dark blue jeans. He thought about his outfit for a long time, as if it might affect Alex's ability to see through him. His guilt is playing tricks on him—whether he turned up in a dark suit, a floral print shirt, or a ski suit, Alex would never guess how their paths had first crossed. How could he? He is focused on a single criminal—the one who left him for dead and is still out there.

Pax is captivated by his mismatched eyes. He expected to find a twisted and disfigured face, but instead the anomaly lends him a unique and heart-rending beauty not unlike his mother's. He turns towards Emi, who's resting against the bookcase. He is incredibly touched to see the way his presence has filled her with hope—it leaves him breathless.

Alex speaks first. He's leaning back slightly, uncomfortable when people get too close.

"Mum says you're an actor?"

"I did a film with Matthew McConaughey, this year," replies Pax. "I really admire him."

Of all the roles he's ever played, this one is the toughest. His heart feels like it's about to beat right out of his chest despite the beta blocker he took earlier. He tries to focus on the details: Alex's T-shirt, which reads "Alive", his unbrushed brown hair, the back of his neck, the elegant line of his shoulders. He gets his delicate physique from his mother.

"It's a Sveberg film. *Don't*," he explains. "Matthew plays a wronged man on a quest for revenge. I play a bartender who becomes his confidant." Embarrassed by his exaggeration, he adds, "It's a small role, but we got on well." Everything seems so fragile—a building under construction that could collapse if he chooses the wrong word. "Matthew taught me an important lesson," continued Pax. "He taught me to listen to my rage. 'In each scene, what's the main emotion? Rage, man. Rage is the one that makes stuff happen', he told me. He said he'd learned it on the set of *Dallas Buyers Club*. Ron Woodroof followed his rage."

He's twisted the facts somewhat. McConaughey didn't share this lesson with him but with the *Telegraph*, in an interview he gave when the film came out. But Pax isn't trying to make himself look good. He just wants to connect with Alex. Last night, he jotted down a hundred quotes and lines by the actor, and re-watched *Dallas Buyers Club*. This time it really affected him since Alex was in the back of his mind throughout. When Woodroof learns his life is over, when he places the gun on his temple to end it; then when he decides to fight, when he finds new meaning in his life.

Alex is a clever young man. He knows the quote was specially chosen for him. After his mother spoke to him about Pax, he thought back to the film as well. He studied the poster still hanging on his wall, where McConaughey holds the motto *Dare to live* in his hands. A fleeting thought suggested to Alex that he might use it to pull himself up and begin moving forward again. Maybe he hadn't chosen it for nothing four years earlier, maybe he had been driven by protective powers, in light of the tragedy that awaited him.

Protective powers? He thought: why me, why me, why me? And he pushed the idea out of his head.

But now Matthew McConaughey is here again, speaking through Pax Monnier, talking to him about rage, a rage that seems nothing like the one he knows, the one that's devouring him. This rage is constructive—a rage for life.

Emi places the tea on the coffee table. Pax sits down to catch his breath and observe Alex in profile. The boy that he . . . That he didn't. That he could have.

He didn't plan for this—for the shock of reality. If he reached out his hand, he could touch the skin, the body that suffered and continues to suffer. A slowed, hindered body. He suddenly wants to throw himself at Alex's feet and beg for forgiveness. But he can't.

He drinks slowly, the spoon rattling in his cup. Why didn't he put it down on the saucer? He breathes in the steam and the tea's faint scent of toasted rice. He doesn't dare look at Emi or her son for fear of betraying his emotions.

"Matthew also says we shouldn't repress our fears. We should speak them out loud," he continues. "He says it's the only way to overcome them."

"What are you afraid of?" asks Alex.

"It's complicated," Pax replies with a sigh. His features tense. "It's hard to say it out loud. Maybe I'll never overcome it after all."

Emi is annoyed. Why is he talking about himself? She was counting on Pax to distract her son from his anxiety, and instead he's dumping his own on her son as well. She remembers when he nearly passed out before their last training session. Then she thinks back to the first time they met, to the rift she'd sensed in him; it had brought them together then, but now it worries her.

"You're talking about stage fright, right, Pax?" she asks in an attempt to change course. "The fear of going on stage to face the camera or an audience?"

She's so far off the mark.

"That's understandable," Alex says softly. "It takes courage to be someone else."

Every word they speak seems to contain ten different meanings, ten arrows, each of which hits its target. The silence grows uncomfortable. Pax wishes he could think of something to say to lighten the atmosphere, but he needs to be alone. He gets up and asks Emi where to find the toilet. As he locks the door, he spies the posters featuring Gilda Texter and Sonia Shimizu on their flashy red Hondas. The unexpected images hit him hard and remind him of *Dallas Buyers Club* yet again—Miss February 1985 sitting on her motorbike in Ron Woodroof's calendar.

When he returns to the lounge, he's got his topic.

"It looks like one of you likes motorbikes!"

"My grandparents had a dealership," replies Alex. "The brunette in the poster is my grandmother, Sonia. She gave me her CB750 for my eighteenth birthday."

He doesn't mention his father, who tacked the posters to the wall but now drives an electric car.

"Wow, nice gift."

"It *was*," replied Alex. "Or, let's say it *could have been*."

Alex grabs a case sitting on the coffee table, pulls out a pair of aviator sunglasses and puts them on. They're too big for him—they accentuate his hollow cheeks.

Of course, thinks Pax. It's Matthew. All he needs now is a cowboy hat.

"Alex doesn't have a driving licence," explains Emi. "He was planning to take the test after his exams—"

Her son cuts her off. "And now I haven't taken my exams or the driving test. The 750 is rusting quietly in the garage. Like its owner, really."

Pax decides to ignore the boy's bitter remark. He sticks to his intuition and his goal of finding something he and Alex can bond over.

"The tyres should still be okay if they were in good condition. You'll need to change the oil, petrol and coolant before starting it again, though. Probably need to replace the oil filter and check the fuses, battery and brakes, too. And clean the air filter. A CB750 deserves respect."

Emi stares at Pax, astonished. His comments take her back to her past, to the garage, to her ex-husband's fascination, to his excitement when he tried out the latest models her parents lent him, to Alex's joyful shouting when Sonia pulled him up onto the motorbike in front of her (Emi was afraid he'd fall off and hurt himself, and was angry with her mother who teased her gently, explaining that she'd never had even the slightest accident in forty years).

"Do you have a motorbike?" she asked.

"Not any more. I had two stolen from me. The last one was a black Virago 1100. I gave up on the idea of buying a third. But I must admit I miss it—the sound of the engine, the speed, the freedom."

Alex smiles. For a brief moment, he joins Pax in a world inaccessible to anyone else. "The way your stomach flies up into your chest, the vibrations that reach your skin through your jacket," he whispers.

"So that's why you wanted to be a pilot," says Pax, more for himself than for the others. "That's what you were looking for: the thrill of acceleration, the feeling of leaving everything behind you, of rising above it all."

He suddenly feels like he's figured Alex out. The root of his motivation and goals. The insurmountable despair of having them taken from him. But at the same time, Pax thinks he can see a way out. Maybe he'll fail, maybe he'll wash up on the beach like an overly confident new swimmer. Only time will tell.

"I could drive it. I could take you out on it, if your mother agrees."

"I'm an adult," replies Alex, without accepting or refusing the offer. "I do as I please."

"There are lots of nice roads around here, through the fields and the woods. That's the great thing about living outside the city. As soon as you put some distance between yourself and the main road or the train station, you're alone. Well, just the two of us, if you agree to ride with me."

Alex lifts his sunglasses to make sure this is all real. He feels like he must be missing something. He runs his hand through his hair to feign nonchalance as he studies his mother's reaction. He knows why she looks worried: he could have an accident, lose his good eye or a limb—he could even die this time. His voluntary self-isolation does have one advantage: Emi always knows her son is safe behind a reinforced door. But she also knows Alex will suffocate if he stays in this flat forever. They both know it. The music he composes and listens to again and again is slowly pulling him further away from the real world. He needs to get out, one way or another, to find his place in the world again, or there will be no future for him.

Emi nods gracefully. "That's a great idea," she says.

Two birds with one stone

That night, they all have trouble falling asleep. They feel like they're walking on a tightrope and can't see the other end. Will it be strong enough to get them across the abyss?

Emi thinks about the decisions she's made. She shouldn't have pushed Alex to get a studio. Though she thought she was acting in his best interests, she created the conditions for the attack. And now, fourteen months later, she's steering his fate again. What if she's wrong?

Images and sounds surround her—sparks fly and metal creaks as the Honda crashes. The sound of bodies falling to the tarmac and being dragged down the street, the fire engines' sirens, the paramedics' hurried footsteps. She's a terrible mother. Then she sees a car overturned in a ditch, smells the blood and earth, hears the sobs of a widow or an orphan. She's a terrible person. She fights to regain control. Her hand reaches towards the drawer of her bedside table where she keeps the morphine, then decides against it. She thinks of Pax and McConaughey. Could speaking her fears out loud really help? Emi gets out of bed and stands in front of the mirror. She opens her mouth—it's harder than she expected. She feels ridiculous and anxious at the same time. She licks her lips, then finally manages to say, "It's not a premonition, it's just your guilt talking. Pax won't take any risks. There won't be a crash. No crash."

*　　*　　*

In his dark room, feverish and exhausted from tossing and turning, Alex gets out of bed and sits down at his desk. With his headphones on, he adds a tight but earthy bassline to a piece he wrote in a hurry earlier. What he feels in the pit of his stomach is overwhelming. He did forget about his blind eye and his self-imposed exile for a moment, though. Pax Monnier reawakened a sensation in him that he'd thought was lost forever. It should be a good thing, but it hurts. It's made him remember the world he's fled and the indescribable joys he once experienced there. Has he let in a Trojan horse? He wonders about Pax's intentions, about the space he plans to take up in his mother's life, which has been exclusively devoted to her son for quite some time. He manages to reason with himself. Emi's well-being is more important than anything else. He accepted Pax's offer of a ride for her sake. If she loves this man, then Alex must try to trust him. Nevertheless, he's not sure he can. It's a huge effort for him to go outside with someone he barely knows. Maybe he's moving too fast. He feels dizzy, sweaty and short of breath. His fingers slip as they move feverishly over the keyboard, but they manage to create a magnificent, unique sound that keeps pace with the beating of his heart. It's the craziest, most intense, most creative sequence he's ever composed.

Pax feels drained as he lies on his bed crying. He's letting it all out. He managed to keep it together, and to avoid lying, but he nearly cracked—and their tea only lasted an hour. What will happen if he spends an entire afternoon with the boy? He's worried, but he doesn't regret his offer. The moment he saw Alex, he knew he would do everything possible to resurrect his will to live. Not because he's Emi's son (though that is obviously a motivating factor), or even because he's the same age as his daughter (while Alex was speaking, he kept seeing Cassandra), but because he likes what he sees in Alex: a deep, complex, striking young man, both lucid and confused, endearing and charismatic. Pax's pain and shame lead his thoughts down some slippery paths: would he feel less of an obligation if the boy were older, or less handsome? If he had a cleft lip instead of different-coloured eyes, or if he loved reality TV "stars" rather than Ron Woodroof and Matthew McConaughey? He sees it as another form of cowardice: empathy only for people you like. But this is stupid, he thinks. I'm happy to accuse myself, but nothing proves I would have behaved differently if Alex had been less interesting. He takes a sleeping pill to shut down his ruminations, but as he drifts off, Alex makes his way into Pax's dreams. What's he really afraid of? Failing to help Alex, or not redeeming himself? Being found out? Losing Emi?

In the morning, when Emi wakes up, she feels lighter. The night has triumphed over her anxiety. She writes a moving text message to Pax, thanking him for finding a way to reach Alex. They know they won't see each other for several days since Pax will be in Nice filming a miniseries he was cast in over the summer.

The time apart acts as a catalyst. Pax turns down dinner invitations from the other cast members to spend his evenings at the hotel studying the CB750 owner's manual. He could take the motorbike to a garage but he's decided to do the tune-up himself. He texts Emi several times a day, since he knows she hates long phone conversations. He sends her postcards, too—something he hasn't done since his divorce. He looks for pictures of the region's natural beauty, or of local flowers, but most of them are ugly and artificially lit, when the light here is truly breathtaking. He decides to get up at dawn to photograph the olive trees and Aleppo pines, and sends them to Emi before heading to work. His only goal is to make her happy. He's seen her smile, but never laugh. He wants to hear her laugh. He's sure Alex is the key: two birds, one stone. His mind is racing. He has no idea how cynical his plan might seem, fixing the son of the woman he loves—the son he helped destroy. He's totally sincere. To survive, he needs to believe that nothing is immutable, that all mistakes can be rectified. If he believes it, it will happen—the power of positive thinking! He phones his daughter to postpone their next dinner (repairing the Honda has become his priority) and to tell her about Emi and Alex: a rushing river of words that pour out into Cassandra's surprised ear. Pax describes Emi's beauty, her grace and remarkable presence. He talks about Alex, "the boy who was assaulted last year and left for dead. Do you remember, Cassandra? Just before the terrible attacks in Marseille and Las Vegas." Cassandra doesn't interrupt him. She's shaken. Of course she remembers. She had identified with the victim and the totally random act of violence had disgusted and terrified her. It meant that anyone could be beaten to death, without any reason—or maybe for twenty euros, but what difference did that make? The assault had taken place in the middle of Paris in broad daylight, not in one of those dodgy suburbs where young people kill each other daily over a look or a joint, one of those areas that the reporters called "no-go zones" and which seemed to her to be on another planet, much like the war in the Middle East. She'd panicked: was violence spreading like an unstoppable virus, making its way across the ring road and into the city? But with her fear came a wash of shame. She suddenly saw herself for what she was—a privileged white girl who lived an easy life free of conflict, poverty, illiteracy, despair and oppression. The murder of two young women the following week by a madman claiming he worked for ISIS had further heightened her feelings of vulnerability, but she hadn't mentioned this to anyone. She'd simply clenched her jaw and prayed for everything to go back to normal. She had focused on her studies and on her father, who seemed unusually anxious. And she succeeded—she returned to her life, to her life as a privileged white woman, just as she had done two years before, following the series of attacks in the capital. She can still see Alex's face, with his green eyes and tousled brown hair, as it appeared on the front page of all the papers. She bombards her father with questions: are any of his injuries permanent? Is the investigation over? She hopes to hear that the assault is little more than a terrible memory that no longer weighs on his mind—what doesn't kill you makes you stronger, as they say—but no, Pax explains, the case is still unsolved and the boy hasn't healed. She feels a sudden rush of admiration when he tells her about his plans to get Alex back on his bike, both figuratively and literally. She'd thought he was obsessed with his career, but now her father seems generous and even selfless. He barely even seems upset by the delayed screening of *Don't*, when just weeks ago he talked about Sveberg's film as if it were a matter of life and death. She enjoys listening to him sounding so determined and committed. At the end of the conversation, she says, "I'm proud of you, Dad."

When he gets back to Paris, Pax finds the overalls and tools he ordered earlier in the week on his doorstep. He's agreed with Emi that he'll go directly to the garage behind the building. Alex won't be joining him: he'll wait until the motorbike is ready.

It's a very cold Saturday and Emi's standing in front of the open garage—a beautiful vision. She's huddled in her thick wool coat, adorned with her artfully tied scarf. She's wearing grey gloves and a simple black felt hat that highlights her exquisite profile, just touching the top of the clip that holds her bun in place. Pax wonders how she always manages to look so elegant without seeming too formal or as though she's in mourning. They haven't seen each other since he came over to meet Alex. Neither of them says a word. She jumps into his arms and he lifts her up. The covered motorbike, an old Civic (an ancient wedding present), a rusted child's bike and a few carefully packed boxes of things Christophe never collected are their only company. Pax wraps himself around Emi and covers her with kisses. He undoes his overalls with his left hand, while the right unbuttons her coat, then removes her gloves and lifts her dress. Her hat falls to the ground, but she doesn't pick it up. He pulls her close and worships her every way he knows how. And she returns the sentiment. As soon as she saw him in the frozen car park, she knew how much she'd missed his body. Everything is on fire: sex, love, reason. It consumes all their doubts, and, when they sit up half naked (no more bun, just tangled black hair, sticky skin, satisfaction, and dust on their necks and shoulders), it takes them a while to realize they're shivering because of the cold, not trembling with pleasure. She puts her things back on, smooths her dress, pulls back her hair. With just four or five quick gestures, she is once again the picture of graceful, almost supernatural beauty.

She smiles and hands the keys to the garage to Pax. "Let me know when you're done."

The motorbike is in perfect condition—it was Sonia's favourite and she took great care of it until she gave it to her grandson. It starts straight away, and it takes just two hours to tune it up. But the autumn days are short: it's already getting dark, so they postpone his outing with Alex until the next day. Pax is pleased, since this means he has more time to ensure he knows the bike inside out. He's ridden plenty of them over the past twenty years, some of which were much more powerful than this one, but he didn't have the same pressure, the same level of responsibility. The stakes are high. If Alex is scared or doesn't trust him, it will be a disaster.

He changes out of the overalls and puts on his leather jacket and helmet. He lifts his leg over the CB750, leaves the car park, and takes the roundabout slowly, then speeds off down a straight road he studied on Google Maps yesterday. The road borders a wood, then the train line that links the suburb to the capital. A train appears, catches up with him, and Pax accelerates, matching its speed until he looks like its escort. There aren't any traffic lights or junctions on the road and the noise from the train drowns out the sound of the motorbike's engine. As the sun sets, they race without spectators, rules or even a finish line.

With his gaze fixed on the horizon, floating somewhere between the earth and sky, Pax screams at the top of his lungs, "Rage is the one that makes stuff happen!"

Through forests and fields

Alex never could have imagined this.

When his mother told him yesterday that Pax would come around 1.30 p.m. to take him for a ride, he thought he wasn't ready—that he'd never be ready. He wished his mother would realize this (actually she had realized, but was feigning ignorance) and cancel. Instead, she simply wished him goodnight. His heart pounded as he listened for sounds outside, hoping for a rainstorm, but in the morning, the roads were dry and the trees still. Now he's heading slowly down the stairs, trying in vain to think of an excuse to go back up to the flat and avoid the situation.

Pax is waiting in front of the glass door to the lobby. Alex is wearing a titanium helmet (supposedly best for absorbing impact) and the black leather jacket and gloves that Sonia gave him with the bike. He's only worn them once before—the day he turned eighteen, when his grandmother had taken him for a ride around the neighbourhood. He didn't enjoy the ride as much as he should have. The day was supposed to be happy and relaxed, but despite his hard work and excellent marks, he was still on the waiting list for a prestigious university and all he remembers feeling is anxiety: would he get in? Getting in was his only goal, and he'd have sacrificed anything for it, but how many others were in the same situation? The school only took the best, the students with the highest marks, and there were plenty of those. How would they make their final selection? They didn't do interviews. A committee read the files and judged the candidates on their personalities and potential as expressed in their covering letters—most of which were actually written by parents who had attended the same prestigious university or one of its competitors, or by expensive admissions coaches, ensuring disturbing levels of legacy admissions. Neither Emi nor Christophe had the right pedigree. Alex had written his letter on his own. It was sincere, but awkward in places, hence his position on the waiting list. At the end of August, he was finally accepted when someone else dropped out at the last minute. He'd spent the entire summer working diligently on his weaker subjects. He can still see himself dropping to his knees, clutching the precious letter to his chest, thanking the heavens for his good fortune—which, although he didn't know it yet, would lead to disaster.

He can't shake this painful memory, which highlights the rampart injustice of the world. Why should he try to glue the pieces of the vase back together since it will still be empty? He's about to turn around when he looks up and sees his mother. She's watching from the window, an encouraging smile on her face.

"Let's go," says Pax.

Alex gets on behind him with little enthusiasm. They've planned a short ride, half an hour at the most. The timing is perfect: the neighbours are busy with their Sunday roasts and the streets are deserted. The Honda travels down a narrow road near the forest, where they cross paths with just a few cars. Alex grips the bike with his legs and holds tightly on to Pax as he accelerates. He stares at the tarmac and whispers to himself that it will be over soon. He doesn't have any expectations, but the cold winter sunlight fills him up as the brisk air sweeps down the back of his neck and into his jacket, wrapping itself around him and invading his lungs, waking him up like a clarion call. He feels shaky. "Are you okay?"

shouts Pax, but his voice is drowned out by the din of the four cylinders. Alex tightens his arms around Pax's waist and squeezes his eyes firmly shut—his mind is fighting it, but a wave of happiness washes over him as the speed makes him feel like a child again. He shakes his head and sticks out his chest, proudly offering it to the wind, then lifts his visor. For the first time since the assault, he wants to live.

They've completed their 35km loop.

"So?" asks Pax as he turns off the engine.

"I dunno," says Alex, still dazed.

What he feels is indescribable.

While Pax takes the motorbike back to the garage, Alex returns to the apartment, carefully takes off his gear, wipes the streaks of dirt off his cheeks and forehead, and smooths down his hair. He'd like to tell his mother, whose eyes are so full of love, that the earth moved beneath him, but he can't find the words. Luckily, Emi doesn't need an explanation. She can tell from the look in his eyes and the way he's moving that he came close to feeling freedom and hope.

She takes his jacket and places it on a wooden hanger. "Pax will be back next Sunday," she says with a smile.

"Sure, why not," he replies.

The following Sunday, Alex wakes at dawn. This time, it has rained, and the ground is covered in wet ochre-coloured leaves. He's not pleased. He studies the cloudy skies, which are clearing too slowly for his liking, afraid his mother might deem the weather conditions too dangerous. When he hears her on the phone to Pax and figures out that their plans are still on, he feels a powerful wave of relief wash over him. At 1.30 p.m., the engine roars. Pax warns him right off the bat: to be safe, the outing will be shorter today. Alex hides his disappointment and climbs onto the 750. With his hips glued to the seat, he leans back to feel the wind on more of his torso without losing his balance. He unzips his jacket, spreads his arms, and gives in to the ecstasy.

He suddenly realizes why he feels so good: he's outside, but still safe.

As long as he's on the bike, no attacker can catch him.

As long as he's moving, no one can hurt him.

The unthinkable happens—Alex wants to keep going, further and faster.

He wants to ride to the next town without slowing or stopping. He wants to keep riding, coming ever closer to the danger, like a wounded soldier drawn to the lights of the battlefield, then moving away again, through forests and fields.

He still doesn't open up to anyone—neither to Pax nor his mother. He returns to his room without a word, his skin and his soul unbelievably alive. He buries his emotions like treasure that could suddenly disappear if he's not careful. He knows all too well how unstable people and events can be.

Emi doesn't mind—the results speak for themselves. The bags under her son's eyes are shrinking. He's sleeping better. His appetite has returned, and so has hers. She plans more outings, happy to be filling the wall calendar in the kitchen with something other than medical appointments. She looks online for long-term weather forecasts, prays for a mild winter, makes sure Pax will be available. He promises he'll be there, that he'll find time outside the weekends to see Cassandra.

"Or maybe, one of these days, we could all spend time together," suggests Emi.

Pax has thought of this before. He wants to—people always enjoy bringing together the people they love. Plus, it might consolidate everything he's built with Alex and Emi, even though the foundation is a lie. It's like with rumours—the more they spread, the truer they become. You fill in the gaps, embellish the details, and it looks so good that the original story disappears altogether. There's no going back. Actually, thinks Pax, the sooner the better—as soon as he's sure Alex feels comfortable with him, he'll organize a lunch for the four of them.

They go on their third ride in early December. Christmas is in the air. The lights on all the balconies remind Alex that the world keeps turning, no matter what. Before he climbs onto the motorbike, he begs Pax to go faster and further. Pax is surprised, but he accepts. He needs it, too. He wants to outrun the thoughts that plague him. The Honda speeds through the frozen countryside, leaning left, then right, rocking Alex into a welcome daze.

With his head thrown back and his eyes closed, the young man gives in to the joy that's taken hold of him. I'm alive, alive, alive, he whispers.

Absolute solitude

When Langlois' secretary told him Emi Shimizu had asked to see him as soon as possible, he imagined the worst. He scheduled an appointment for her the same day. Several times, during sessions with other patients, his mind wandered to Emi, pondering different possibilities. Had Alex's condition worsened, pulling Emi down with him? Had Emi finally given in to disappointment and despair? He'd often noticed that following a death or any other type of tragedy, it's a while before patients fall apart. Right after the event, people are surrounded by shoulders to cry on, they have pharmaceutical help, and they seem to be all right. But little by little, as their support system dwindles, their mental health declines amid general indifference.

Langlois never imagined that Emi was actually doing better. Later, when he thought back to this moment, he realized how pessimistic he'd been. Of course this was partly due to his work—he mostly saw lost, hopelessly depressed people—but he'd also been influenced by the trend he'd noticed months earlier: the rise in violence. It had continued to spread, change and grow, and it was really getting to him. Hate crimes by homophobes, racists, misogynists and anti-Semites, assaults with absolutely no motive, public health scandals, the threat of extremism growing everywhere in Europe, religion as politics, and most recently the desperate Yellow Vests movement ripping through the country.

Langlois was wrong: Emi Shimizu smiles as she steps into his office. Both her movements and her gaze seem lighter. She's come to tell him he was right to promise her there were better days ahead. She's met someone, a man, who has changed everything. She tells him how they clicked immediately, and about the connection between Pax, Alex, McConaughey, and the Honda. She tells him about the first signs of improvement in her son, which his psychiatrist has confirmed, deciding not to up his medications. Langlois is pensive. He knows that people do sometimes jump the gun, but he feels that declaring someone your soulmate in just a few weeks, after such a long period of unhappiness, is a bit hasty. He would really love to meet this exceptional man (the adjective comes with doubt-filled quotation marks in his head).

"I'm happy for you, Ms Shimizu, but you didn't need a same-day appointment to tell me you're feeling better."

"I need your help," replied Emi. "Yours or someone else's. I've been taking morphine for nearly three months now. I suppose giving it up shouldn't be impossible, since I haven't been using for very long, but I can tell it won't be easy."

Langlois is speechless, shaken to the core. He had no idea; he hadn't noticed a thing. He immediately thinks of Mikhail Bulgakov, whose work he has always admired.

"Now you know," continues Emi. "I know the morphine is dragging me down just as much as it's helping me get through. I've reached the point where it's starting to be the one in control, not me."

"It's a shame you've waited till now to tell me," Langlois says before he can stop himself. He's irritated with her. He's suddenly realized that she's only ever revealed a tiny fragment of herself to him. What good is he if she can't be honest with him? Some psychologists would have sent her away immediately. But he can't—his resentment has already given way to concern. Of course he'll help her. He has no intention of watching Emi Shimizu self-destruct—not when she's found hope again. He looks through his address book and scribbles the name and phone number of an addiction specialist on a Post-it, which he hands to her.

Emi thanks him and stands to leave. "It's not that I don't want to tell you certain things," she says. "It's that I don't know how."

That's the truth. She knows how to build fortresses, walls and levees, but she doesn't know how to take them down and let it all out.

As soon as his patient has gone, Langlois looks for his copy of *Morphine* in his bookcase, on a hunt for a sentence that struck him when he read it, but that he can't quite remember now. "For an addict there is one pleasure of which no one can deprive him—his ability to spend his time in absolute solitude. And solitude means deep, significant thought; it means calm, contemplation—and wisdom." The description is striking—it could be a portrait of Emi Shimizu. She must have gone looking for something in the morphine that she could no longer produce herself. Now she can finally see and fear the danger. She doesn't want the "pleasure" any more. She no longer wants to live in absolute solitude. All thanks to this man, this Pax Monnier. I do hope, thinks Langlois, that she'll retain her wisdom and calm.

War dog

It's almost winter. Others see it as a threat, but Emi Shimizu sees only its beauty. Every morning, she opens the thick curtains that darken her room and watches the changing sky, the naked branches, the migrating flocks and the winter shadows. She thinks of the scene as compensation for waking up alone in her bed—it's still too soon to leave Alex alone at night or have Pax stay over.

The Thea & Co. training at Demeson is over. Pax and Emi do their best to synchronize their diaries. Sometimes they manage lunch together, or he drops by in the late afternoon. They have an early dinner together two or three times a week, since the train she takes home is said to be dangerous late at night. They don't talk much. Instead they enjoy a companionable silence. They spend hours lying next to each other. She is filled with gratitude and he with wonder. They're both surprised by their love, by this happy development in their lives. Sometimes a news story, an image or a sound takes Pax back to his memories of 23 September 2017, but he's learned to block it out, to push it away, to compartmentalize. He's come up with an effective story to protect himself: he didn't attack Alex. It's true he could have saved his eye, but the real damage—the boy's withdrawal from the world and the insidious terror that plagues him—is someone else's fault. Pax has begun to believe Emi when she says he has pulled her son back from the brink, that he's an amazing guy. Does he have any other choice?

Alex is showing signs of life. He goes into his mother's room and looks in the mirror. He no longer cries tears of rage at the sight of his mismatched eyes. He studies them, trying hard to make their strangeness his own. He cuts a few inches off his hair, to make wearing the helmet more comfortable. He asks his physiotherapist for more exercises to make his legs, arms and back stronger. He hasn't told anyone what he's planning, because he still wonders if this can all be real, but for the first time since the assault, he has a goal: he's going to get his motorbike licence. He's looked online, and it seems one eye should be enough. He'll drive the Honda—his Honda. Until then, he'll enjoy the sensation while riding behind Pax. He lets his guard down, little by little. He has to admit that Pax seems sincerely invested in him and his mother. What Alex likes most is how Pax is the exact opposite of his father. He doesn't talk about an improbable future filled with tennis lessons and all-inclusive holidays. He doesn't serve up annoyingly critical speeches that always begin with "You have to": "You have to get out more", "You have to move on", "You have to be strong". He doesn't offer any advice or order him around. He brings his DVDs with him, and after their rides, they watch McConaughey films until it gets dark, discussing their meaning and the soundtracks.

Sometimes they laugh together. Sometimes they high five each other.

Alex doesn't know it yet, but he's about to shed his armour; it's no longer a shield but a burden.

It happens on a Sunday afternoon when Pax steps into the flat. His phone rings: it's Cassandra. He forgot to postpone their plans, and she's been waiting outside his building for fifteen minutes.

"I'm really sorry," he says. "I've just got to Emi's. Can we meet up tomorrow instead?"

"Or," Alex interrupts, "Cassandra could come here. We can go for a ride while she's on the train. Mum's made mochis."

Alex himself is more surprised by his suggestion than anyone else. He hasn't socialized with anyone under the age of forty for nearly fifteen months. That's been his choice, and he's stuck to it. But this time, it's different. He's desperate to spend time with someone his age. He can feel it in his body, somewhere between his stomach and his lungs, like the need for sunlight after a long winter. So he takes advantage of the situation. Meeting Cassandra is relatively low risk. He won't have to talk about his past, like he would do with his former classmates. She won't bring up any unwanted memories. And, if he's overestimated what he can manage, if it's too much, if she asks questions he can't answer, he can always slip away to his room.

Meeting Cassandra today is the perfect occasion to try building a bridge back to the world.

"So, what did she say?" asks Emi, trembling, when Pax hangs up.

"She's coming, of course," replies Pax.

He's a bit nervous. Cassandra is a volcano, always on the verge of erupting. She's only twenty-four, that age when young people think they know how the world works, when they don't mind making mistakes because they're sure they'll always find a way to start again. He warns Emi and Alex that his daughter always says what she thinks—sometimes without enough consideration for others.

"That sounds perfect," replies Alex. "Come on, let's go on that ride before she gets here."

Christmas is only a few days away. The roads are full of last-minute shoppers on the hunt for gifts.

They've been out for about ten minutes when they find

themselves boxed in by cars on either side, on their way to a shopping centre. A thirty-something man in one of them stares at Alex. Pax doesn't notice. He's just an ordinary guy wondering whether he should give his sister a pair of earrings or some perfume, whose gaze happened to fall on Alex.

But Alex doesn't know that.

The fear is there, ready to go for the jugular, like a war dog.

He pulls on Pax's shoulder, nearly causing them to topple over.

"I'm cold," he stutters. "Let's go back."

Woman Worldwide

Later, Pax will think back to that moment as the warning sign before the tsunami. An unassuming little wave, which immediately dissipated, leaving nothing behind but the calm, flat sea glimmering in the sunlight.

Cassandra was that calm sea.

The young woman shakes Emi's hand and finds her even more beautiful in person than on the photo Pax has shown her. The gentle kindness she exudes wins Cassandra over, reassuring her about her father's choice. She kisses Alex hello on both cheeks   something no one has been able to do since the assault. As his mother looks on, holding her breath, he does the same, without even knowing why. Pax's daughter doesn't wait for an invitation to sit down, but her buoyant mood makes up for the faux pas. She's spontaneous, talkative and clearly determined to do what she can to help Alex recover.

The parents disappear into the kitchen so the children can talk freely.

Cassandra has an idea. Pax has told her that Alex spends most of his time composing, so music will be her way in—she loves it. She and Ingrid go to festivals all over Europe to dance the night away. She always has headphones on and spends hours looking for new discoveries on the internet. That should be plenty to keep the conversation going and bring them together. Alex might keep up with new releases, but nothing can replace the chatter heard in concert venues, university corridors and bars where young people meet to catch up over a drink. She can offer him vicarious access to the world outside. She thinks of what she's doing as a mission, but as soon as they start talking, she realizes it's fun. He's not especially talkative, but he's deep and charming in a way that helps Cassandra forget what happened to him.

"What have you been listening to lately?" she asks.

Alex studies her as if she were a painting with multiple possible interpretations.

"I've been really into the *Woman Worldwide* album by Justice," she continues. "I can't get it out of my head."

She starts singing. It's not premeditated—the lyrics are in her head all day every day, in the metro, in the bus, while she's getting ready . . . They come to her unbidden: "By the laws of attraction, and the rules of the game, there's a chemical reaction, between pleasure and pain . . ."

"Use imagination as a destination. Use imagination as a destination and come closer. Forever," Alex jumps in for the chorus.

Perfectly in sync, they stop, both surprised by their improvised duet. Justice! She suddenly realizes that she could have chosen a band with a more appropriate name, but the lyrics couldn't have been more apposite.

Emi and Pax are frozen in the doorway, their arms laden with cakes and a tray of tea and soft drinks. They don't dare move.

"I love that song," says Alex. "It looks like we have similar taste in music."

"Yeah, let's see," she says as she pulls her phone out of her handbag, hands him the headphones, and chooses a track.

Alex begins to relax. He realizes, of course, that it's easier to feel normal within the confines of his safe flat, on the island that is his building, than it is on the 750, watched by strangers. But he'd nearly forgotten this feeling of being in the right place at the right time—in fact, he's not sure he's ever really experienced it before. His hand bounces to the beat on the sofa's armrest.

"Now it's your turn," declares Cassandra. "Dad tells me you compose music. Can I listen to one of your tracks?"

He composes, sure, but with no goals or expectations. Music is his sanctuary. He uses it to express his anger and confusion, to give form to his hallucinations. It liberates him. He has never imagined letting anyone else in.

Nevertheless, he nods, stands up, and leads Cassandra to his room. She takes in his world: the smell of darkness, McConaughey and the *Dare to live* poster, the Ray-Ban sunglasses on the bedside table, the jeans and T-shirt crumpled on the floor, the record player, the shelves of records, the computer, the keyboard. She looks instinctively for textbooks, a diary, a calculator, but there are no traces of the student he used to be. This painful realization reminds her of how random and cruel fate can be. Her own room is full of papers and exercise books, her weekly planner tacked to the wall, CVs, and covering letter drafts for her applications to foreign MBA programmes. She's known Alex for less than an hour, but she already wants to hug him like a brother.

"Sit," says Alex, gesturing towards the only chair.

He makes a few adjustments and presses play. Cassandra has planned to exaggerate her enjoyment, though she doesn't think she'll have to lie. She's certain she'll like what he's written, and she'll express interest in his work to prove to him he exists. She expects to hear something a little derivative, a blend of recycled influences, and it will probably be depressing, but she's sure it will have some positive qualities. Instead, she's confronted with a totally new sound. It's bright and powerful. The bassline transports her, sparking her senses. She opens her eyes wide. Where did this kid come from?

How did he come up with these beats, these harmonies, these otherworldly choruses?

When she takes off the headphones, her face is transformed. "You can't keep this to yourself. It's amazing! Music needs to be out there in the world. Let me take care of it."

Alex is surprised. He's never really thought of his music as good or bad. It's like the blood coursing through his veins or the air in his lungs. It fills him, nourishes him, eases his pain.

"You're an artist," she continues. "This song could make the dead get up and dance!" Something tells her she needs to push him. It's her secret strength—Cassandra never holds back. She's not afraid to fail, but she is terrified of regrets.

"I don't want to have to meet anyone," says Alex, giving in. "No one at all."

"No need."

When she gets back to Paris, she sends the song to one of her friends, who has a major YouTube music channel and an account on SoundCloud.

The first week, it gets 100,000 views. The second, nearly 180,000.

Merry Christmas

This year, Alex has had to agree to spend Christmas at his father's. He's only seen him a handful of times over the past year, and Christophe left every single one of his visits annoyed by his older son's lack of interest in his new little brother (he just looked at the pictures without a word, and the kid was really cute!). But this time, he thinks, it will be different. Alex will be at his place, on his home turf. Christophe has cleared out his office and put in a bed so his eldest son can have his space. He'll realize how warm and welcoming this family is: *they* don't spend their time meditating around incense burners; *their* home is not an oppressive, silent temple. It's filled with joy: a Christmas tree decorated with multicoloured baubles and gold tinsel, fake frost on the windows, knitted stockings over the fireplace, and a thick, beige rug.

As they sit down for drinks on Christmas Eve, Christophe raises his champagne flute with a wink at his wife, Pauline. "To offers that can't be refused!"

Alex looks at him, confused.

"This is our gift," continues Christophe. "Pauline and I want to expand the firm. We'll need more administrative staff, and we thought of you."

"You can work from home at first, if you prefer," adds Pauline. "But with a proper salary."

"You need to move on. You're doing much better, and nothing more can be done for your eye, right? Holing yourself up at your mother's isn't doing you any favours, son!"

Alex cannot stand this term of "endearment".

"Fifteen months is long enough, I think. The assault was terrible. It ruined all your plans, but you're strong! You have plenty of willpower—you proved that time and again in school, working all hours! So, use it, son. It's not the life you planned on, but you can still make something of it."

Alex is confused. Is his father trying to help him, or just trying to get revenge on his ex-wife by showing her he still has a few cards up his sleeve? The truth is, he does have good intentions. The birth of his second son reminded Christophe of his duties and responsibilities. He wants to show Pauline that he's a good father—and to prove it to himself. But he's never asked himself the right questions. He's never tried to understand how Alex feels. He has asked his son about Emi's love life (and was shocked to learn of Pax's existence), but never about his feelings—his desires, his pain, his frustrations. Not a word. Christophe superimposes his own view of events on his son. He pretends not to see the distance between them, and he behaves as if the past doesn't matter.

"Thanks, Dad, but I'm not really interested in the property business."

"Oh really? Well what are you interested in?" asks Christophe. "This is real life, son. I'm talking about your future. A career. A path to being an independent adult. Have you heard anything about your application for disability allowance? You'll probably get a decent sum. Which you deserve, of course, given what you've been through! At least your handicap comes with a few advantages, including lower social contributions for your employer . . ."

"I'm going to take my motorbike test this summer."

Christophe turns to Pauline and shakes his head, as if apologizing for his son's lack of gratitude.

"Your motorbike test? Do you really think that's a good idea?"

Alex doesn't understand. He finally has a goal, a date on his calendar. It's taken a huge amount of effort to get this far, and he'd expected an enthusiastic and encouraging reaction. My father doesn't understand anything, nothing at all, he thinks. The feeling of his arms around Pax's waist on the back of the Honda helps steady him.

"Well, I can still change my mind," he lies.

"Well let's hope you do. And give our offer some thought!"

Dinner—oysters on the half-shell and pan-seared foie gras, which Alex hardly touches—ends early. Everyone's tired, since the baby tends to wake at dawn, and another even more festive meal will be served tomorrow.

Alex sleeps badly. The mattress is comfortable, and Pauline chose nice grey cotton linen and a big, fluffy towel, but all Alex can see is the rest: a collection of tennis trophies (and now golf as well) his father has won, files on the buildings he's selling flats in ("Hornbeam", "Oak Alley", "Poplar Lane"—he wonders if there's a paragraph in the terms and conditions requiring two poplars to be planted at the entrance to justify the name), family pictures of Christophe, Pauline and the baby in front of the country house, with its huge blue hydrangeas—a family not his own.

When the little boy's cries pull Alex from sleep, it's nearly noon. His joints hurt and his chest feels tight, even when he takes slow, deep breaths. He's ready for the day to be over, to go back to his room at home, his computer, his keyboard and his headphones. He gets dressed quickly and pads to the kitchen, where Pauline is cooking the turkey. He doesn't go through the dining room, where he would have seen an extra place setting at the table.

"Where's my dad?" he asks.

"He's picking up a few things. He'll be back any minute with fresh bread and the cake. Have some coffee. I'm going to change your brother and get him dressed. We'll put him in the highchair with us at the table—he loves it."

Her upbeat tone disguises her misgivings perfectly. She discussed it with Christophe at length—they disagreed about this lunch, but she gave in, since he was Alex's father after all. He must know best.

Alex sits down in the lounge. There's a documentary on TV, but he pays no attention to it. He gulps his coffee. The front door opens just as he puts down his cup. A bearded stranger walks in wearing a black hoodie, a bottle of wine in his hand.

"Ah, at last we meet," he says affably.

What happens next takes only four or five seconds. Alex jumps up from his chair. Everything he's learned or come to understand has disappeared. His ability to reason is suspended as a thick blanket of panic smothers his brain. He picks up one of the golf clubs on display and, full of rage, lets out a terrifying grunt and hits the man as hard as he can (luckily, not very hard), aiming for his head.

The man tries to dodge the blow, but the club hits his shoulder, making him drop the bottle, which shatters on impact with the corner of a piece of furniture. The wine spreads to the beige rug, leaving a dark purple stain. He steps back, horrified.

"What the hell is wrong with you?" he shouts.

Alex's whole body is shaking. The walls seem to be spinning, and there's no air left in the room. He lifts his arms to deliver a second blow but instead collapses onto the sofa.

Christophe stands stock still in the doorway. He's carrying a cake box and two baguettes. Pauline has run over, crying, holding her screaming son tight in her arms. The baby can feel the tension coming off his parents, and especially his uncle, whose collarbone is broken.

"This is my brother, Alex. My brother Benoît."

Christophe will remember this Christmas for a long time. Pauline will bring it up for years: she told him he should have let Alex know Benoît was coming, but he wanted to surprise him—and how. Christophe still believes Alex would have refused to have another guest if he'd been given the choice, so he felt it was better not to ask. The boy needed to move on, after all. He admits the real mistake was asking Benoît to open the door since his hands were full. He had overestimated his son's ability to behave normally.

While driving Alex back to his mother's, he can't stop thinking, Benoît is right, my son is a psycho, he's lost it. He feels a combination of pity and annoyance. Alex lacks drive and motivation. Christ, fifteen months is long enough, isn't it?

Christophe forgets that when he was Alex's age, he didn't have any drive. He also forgets that the most traumatic event he's ever had to face was a hot-air balloon ride at the age of ten (he had to lie down to keep from seeing the empty space below him). He's never been in danger and the most physical pain he's ever experienced was at the dental clinic, or maybe once when he sprained his ankle skiing. But that doesn't stop him from judging his son, underestimating his pain, and reducing his tragedy to a minor incident.

Emi is waiting for them in front of the apartment building, distraught.

"This is a big deal. Do you realize Benoît could press charges against your son? What the hell is that psychiatrist playing at? Honestly, it's beyond me. Especially since he doesn't even remember it!"

"He knows what he went through. His body remembers, even if his mind doesn't. He panicked. It was an accident, Christophe. Can't you understand that?"

"What I understand is that you're smothering him. You have to dive in to realize you can swim."

"Maybe," replies Emi as Christophe gets back in the car. "Thank you for everything and Merry Christmas."

The world is upside down

Once she knows Alex is safe in his room, Emi puts on her coat, laces her hiking boots, and runs to the forest. The carpet of decomposing leaves gives way under her feet. She picks up pieces of fallen brown tree bark and crumbles them in her hands, then looks up towards the canopy of trees in search of comfort, but finds only a hostile maze of bare branches. A clammy, unknown fear is setting in. She adjusts her scarf, turns back, and calls Pax.

She gets his voicemail. He has turned off his phone to spend an uninterrupted day with Cassandra. His daughter has just told him something extraordinary: a record label is interested in signing Alex. How many young musicians dream of this moment!

As Emi gives in to her despair, Cassandra traces a new future for Alex. Pax is dumbfounded—he only uses YouTube to watch trailers and has no idea what 100,000 or 200,000 views means in terms of advertising revenue, exposure and influence. Alex will sign a contract and receive an advance to buy the material he needs to produce an album. It will be a whole new life. It's not a miracle, just the result of hard work and talent.

Pax studies his daughter. Her determination and quick thinking impress him. If her plan works, a huge door will open for Alex. A way out and up that won't give him back his eye, but will give him the chance to feel pride and happiness again. It won't change what Pax did—the cowardice and the shame—but it would be a huge relief. He imagines Alex happy and relaxed.

"He's really talented, Dad. He thought he was destined to become a pilot, but that would have been a waste! He'll go much further and higher as a composer than he would have in a plane."

She's right. Alex has found a freedom in music that he didn't even know existed. It channels the feeling that he's suffocating, or on fire, or that the world is upside down into his songs, calming his muddled thoughts. With his headphones on, Alex can defeat his personal hell.

"That's fantastic, Cassandra. But he barely leaves the house and you're talking about going on tour?"

"Be positive, Dad. He's improving quickly. And it's all thanks to you!"

"Me?"

"The motorbike, Dad. He's ventured back out into the world, and it's only the beginning. Don't worry about the tour yet, it won't happen right away. It's a long-term goal, but that's the key. You know better than most people how important those can be, right? Think of Sveberg!"

Pax smiles sadly. "There is no more Sveberg, Cassandra. No more film. He cut my character in the edits."

"Oh, Dad."

"It doesn't matter any more. Happens to the best of us, right?"

"A year ago, you were talking about it like it was a matter of life and death."

When Pax listened to Gaspard's awkward explanation a few weeks earlier, he didn't think about his career—he thought about Alex. About the life the boy had planned for himself versus the harsh reality. Sure, being cut from the film hurt a little, but less than he would have thought. He wasn't sure whether to interpret the turn of events as the punishment he deserved, or simply as a sad waste.

The next day is a Sunday, and he's scheduled to go for a ride with Alex. He remembers the feeling of letting his dreams dissolve into the frozen tarmac as they sped down the road.

"Things happen that change our priorities," he replies. "Speaking of which, have you told Alex about all this?"

"I sent him an email, but he hasn't replied. I guess he's celebrating Christmas with his family."

"I'm going to call Emi," Pax says as he turns on his phone. "She'll be so delighted."

The screen tells him he has six missed calls and a voice message.

"I think she must already know," he says with a smile as he hits play on the message. Then his face falls.

"I need you, Pax. I need you."

The wave

Emi Shimizu has never said those words before. She has never relied on anyone to pick her up when she stumbles. She didn't start seeing Langlois by choice—she was just following the hospital's advice. And she never really told him anything. She learned from a very young age how to build walls to protect herself, having realized, without harbouring any resentment about it, that her parents, her friends, and even Christophe when they were together, loved her without understanding her. And she's managed fine on her own until today, until this tsunami that nothing, not even morphine, can hold back. The wave is looming over her, ready to swallow her and her son whole—and she thinks of Pax.

She thinks of everything he's already done for them. The overwhelming power of their love. She needs him. Without him, the wave will pull her under.

"I'm here. Of course I'm here. I'll always be here for you," he reassures her over the phone.

"I'm on my way," she replies.

She slips a note under Alex's door to let him know she'll be gone for a few hours and hurries to the garage to the old Honda Civic. She refuses to depend on public transport tonight.

Pax asks Cassandra to go, without any explanation. Luckily his daughter can tell he's preoccupied and tactfully takes her leave.

The minutes feel like centuries as he waits.

When she finally arrives, she throws herself into his arms. They stay that way for a long time, locked together, in silence. She's overwhelmed by anxiety and emotion; he's consumed with worry. But then the words begin to flow. She tells Pax about Alex's violent reaction, the impenetrable look she saw on his face when he locked himself in his room, all these steps backwards when Emi thought he was finally moving on. How naive: she knows full well that people can never truly escape uncertainty.

It's humanity's curse, our inability to know the truth. It's what kills us—knowing that the truth is there, but out of reach.

"I was so sure he was doing better," whispers Pax, shocked. "Everything seemed to be going well. He was planning on getting his motorbike licence! And his music! Your son is talented, Emi. Cassandra told me earlier that a record label wants to sign him."

"It's all a fantasy. Alex will never get better, and neither will I. That's what I finally realized this afternoon. My son will live the rest of his life with that savagery in him, that irrational fear of others, of a threat looming over him, wherever he is."

Pax pulls her closer to his chest. Her body is soft, as if filled with tears. "You'll get through this, Emi. Time heals all wounds."

"Time heals . . . That's all a fairy tale," she replies bitterly. "You think you're safe, but then it all comes crashing down on you again. It's all crashing down on me, Pax. I'm not as tough as I thought, and my son is broken. You know what the worst part is, though? His attacker might already be behind bars. If we'd just been a bit luckier, everything could have been different. Alex would have been able to put it behind him."

"What are you talking about?"

"They arrested a man a few months ago. He'd assaulted

another boy in his flat, beating him to death. Just like with Alex, there was no motive, it was the same MO, same weapon—brass knuckles. This time the police conducted a more in-depth investigation, since the victim died. They found fingerprints. He's in jail, awaiting trial."

The air grows thin around Pax. He gets up and opens the window, despite the cold.

"The detectives linked it to our case. Everything matches, absolutely everything. But Alex doesn't remember anything at all, and there were no witnesses, no evidence. So we're stuck with the uncertainty."

She turns around to find Pax leaning over the window railing. "Pax?"

He stands up straight and staggers back over to the sofa.

"Come here," he whispers, holding out his arms. "Life is so unfair, it's true."

She buries her face in his shoulder and feels instantly comforted.

The chance of a lifetime

Everything is exploding in Pax. Flesh, cells, organs and thoughts collide. He feels like his eyes are trying to pop out of their sockets—probably because they don't want to revisit the image he's retained from 23 September 2017: a massive back, a brown leather jacket, and short blond hair with an unattractive bald spot at the nape of the neck.

The wave hovers over his head, ready to drown him. He looks up at it, sees that it's made up of his lies, regrets and mistakes.

Most people would flee. But can he? Does he even want to?

Pax may hold Alex's fate in his hands. Until now, his statement would have revealed the truth, but it would have made no difference to the boy. However, now that the suspect has been arrested and his second crime proven, it could change everything. If he's a broad-shouldered blond guy who's losing his hair, Pax's statement could get him convicted for Alex's assault, too. First, Pax must make sure that this is definitely the case—but even doing that much means pushing the self-destruct button on his life.

He holds a business card in his hand. It belongs to the police officer whom he met fifteen months ago. The corners are worn and dirty from spending all that time in his wallet. Pax can still see his jaded expression at the lift, when he said, "The world is just full of maniacs . . ."

His entire body is shaking. If he talks and the image from his memory links the suspect to the assault, the uncertainty will be lifted for Alex, putting an end to his nightmare. He'll finally know the name of his assailant and will know he's behind bars. He won't have to scan the shadows, watch everyone's movements, or analyse the noises in his apartment building lobby any more. He'll find his way back to hope, and Emi will find peace. But the trade-off is terrifying.

He thinks long and hard before reaching his conclusion. How would he react if their roles were reversed? He puts himself in Emi's, Alex's and Cassandra's shoes one by one— all he feels is disgust and horror.

He's certain they'll all see him for what he really is: a selfish, cowardly liar.

He considers keeping quiet, and runs through the arguments in favour of that choice. Firstly, he didn't see the attacker's face, and although he's not a cop or a barrister, he thinks that might well make his testimony inadmissible. Secondly, even if he can't be formally sentenced for Alex's assault, the similarities in MO have already incriminated his attacker, and he's in jail. Alex is safe, and that's the main thing. Thirdly, would Alex really recover as Emi thinks he would just by learning his attacker's identity? Pax has his doubts. The assault has scarred Alex both physically and emotionally. He'll live the rest of his life with the knowledge that violence can suddenly appear any time, anywhere. And lastly, Pax will lose all the people he loves. Forever. He'll lose them, he'll lose them, he'll lose them.

He'll lose them.

Nausea washes over him.

The feeling he has on the bike, Alex's arms around his waist, the glint in his eyes.

Emi's kisses, her hair loose on the back of her neck, her grace and bravery.

Cassandra's smile, her kind words, *I'm proud of you, Dad.*

No, thinks Pax. I can't add this lie to all the others. Back then, I could explain why I ignored things that 23 September: there was the pressure from Sveberg, *Don't*, the chance of a lifetime. Now, I'm all out of excuses. There's no more role to go after, no more glory to claim. There are only two weights on the scale: on one side, the brutal truth, honour, and the end of happiness; on the other, contentment, shame, and betrayal.

What are Emi's love and kindness, Alex's trust, and Cassandra's admiration worth if he doesn't deserve them?

What is *he* worth?

Identification

A new witness expressed his desire to testify in the [. . .] case. We took his statement (below) at [. . .] station.

Identification: "My name is Émile Moreau, but I use the alias Pax Monnier. I was born [. . .] and live [. . .]"

Testimony: "[. . .] On Saturday 23 September 2017, I was home between 4.25 p.m. and 4.35 p.m. I am certain of the exact time because I had a meeting at the Lutetia Hotel at 5 p.m. with Peter Sveberg, and I had carefully calculated my itinerary from the office where I had been working, which I left at 4 p.m., to my place, where I wanted to change my clothes, and then on to the Lutetia. I heard suspicious noises coming from the second-floor flat, but I was overwhelmed by the stress of my audition and didn't want to be late, so I convinced myself it wasn't anything serious and left. That's when I saw a man running down the stairs and out of the building. He was tall with very broad shoulders and was wearing a brown leather jacket. He was blond, with short hair, and a strange bald spot at the nape of his neck shaped like a semicircle. I remember this detail because usually people lose their hair at the crown first. When I was summoned to testify on Monday 25 September 2017, I didn't think that what I'd seen would help to identify the attacker. I was also afraid I might make a mistake and incriminate an innocent man, and I didn't want to get into any trouble. I was afraid I might be charged with something for failing to intervene. I panicked. That's why I told the officer that day that I was home at 4 p.m., so I would be left alone. Later, I learned that the crime was still unsolved because there was no physical evidence and the victim was suffering from amnesia. That convinced me that I'd made the right decision because my statement wouldn't have changed anything.

But I've come back today because I recently learned that a suspect has been arrested for a similar crime, with a nearly identical MO to the Winckler case. I got this information from the victim's mother, whom I met through work. I realized that if my description matches this suspect, you may be able to convict him for the assault of Alex Winckler as well. I regret not intervening when I heard all that noise."

"It's not a bald spot," mumbles the officer. "It's alopecia. And it's a perfect match."

Save me from eternity

Is betrayal less painful when there's someone there to share it with you?

Pax certainly hopes so. He asked Cassandra to come with him to Emi's, implying that Alex needs her support following the incident at his father's. Now that they're all together, he gazes at each of them in turn, trying to drink in the sight of his loved ones before they turn their backs on him. He's a man watching his house burn down, powerless to do anything about it.

Emi's wearing a blue silk and wool dress with a thin gold chain and Mary Jane shoes. Her hair is up in a bun, held in place by a lacquered wooden stick. Brown eyeliner emphasizes her eyes, and she's put on pale pink blusher to mask her fatigue. She forces a smile as she pours the tea into small white bowls, studying her son's expressions. He's spent the past three days locked in his room, but he agreed to come out when she told him Pax and Cassandra were coming.

Emi doesn't know that the truth is sitting right next to her. Her son will soon be rid of the uncertainty that plagues him. He will have answers to the questions surrounding his attack and be free to think about his future again. As will she, once she gets over the initial shock and finds a way to recover from the pain. In a few hours, she'll draft her resignation letter. She'll make an appointment with the HR manager next week and explain that she no longer feels she has a place at Demeson. He'll say he's sorry to lose her and tell her she did excellent work for them, particularly since the accident, with that theatre training. She'll suggest they stop anonymizing Christian Perraud by using initials in memos about his death, and that they review their support programme for employees nearing retirement age (and she'll know from the executive's polite nod that he won't change a thing). When she leaves, she'll pass on her files, except for the archived email, which she'll permanently delete. Christian Perraud's prophecy has come to pass: she won't be forgetting him any time soon. The uncertainty will continue to eat away at her. It will ease off occasionally, but then, when she hears about an incident on the news or in a discussion with colleagues, whenever there's a workers' strike, it will return with a vengeance. If Emi had opened that email sooner, if she'd met with Christian Perraud and listened to what he had to say, she would have understood that he never planned to end his life. He wasn't depressed; he was angry. He was ready to go head-to-head. He knew enough about the company's violations to take action against them, maybe even win a court case. But then the steering wheel slipped, and his revenge was stolen from him—nothing can escape the whims of fate.

Cassandra is wearing a pretty beige jumper, jeans and black ankle boots. She's sitting on the sofa armrest talking to Alex, who's standing with his back against the wall. She's telling him about the record deal that's in the works, and the number of YouTube views, which keeps going up. Alex doesn't answer. He's sullen and aloof, but Cassandra doesn't give up easily. Her determination and endless energy are her best qualities. She winks at her father as if to say, "Don't worry, I've got a handle on it." In ten minutes, she'll be speechless, stunned by the revelation that will shake the ground beneath them all. She'll be terribly ashamed of her father. Later tonight she'll cry tears of rage as she struggles to fall asleep. But she won't be thinking of him or Alex; she'll be thinking of Ingrid, sleeping next to her. Cassandra has met another woman. It's been a month already, a month since she was swept off her feet. The feeling is so strong that she knows she has to break up with her girlfriend. She hasn't said anything, though. She's in the final stages of the admissions process for a prestigious MBA in New York—the goal she's been working towards since September. It's not the right time for a split.

Alex bites his lip as he listens to Cassandra go on about albums, success and future plans. She must be talking about someone else, some guy who has it all. He thinks about the track he composed yesterday, "Save me from eternity"; about the giant hole inside him that's tearing him apart, and which grew even larger at Christmas. He thinks life must have made a mistake by offering to love him again. He won't be made a fool of twice. And yet, that's exactly what's about to happen: a few words will soon change everything.

Pax contemplates the three people who matter most to him and feels his heart contract, pulling on his lungs.

He can't breathe.

"Pax," says Emi, worried. "Is something wrong? Say something!"

All is said

All is said.

They're all standing across from him, frozen in shock.

Cassandra reacts first. She shoots her father a furious look, picks up her coat and scarf, puts her gloves on her trembling fingers, kisses Alex goodbye on both cheeks, thinks about saying something to him, but changes her mind and leaves.

Emi remains silent. She stares at Pax Monnier, or maybe it's Émile Morcau. She doesn't really know who he is any more. There are no words to describe how she feels. She finally tears her gaze away from this man she . . . this man who . . . and runs to the bathroom. She falls to her knees without a sound, like she did on 23 September 2017, beside her son's body.

Pax slowly gathers his things and leaves, his feet stamping out the ashes of his charred and blackened dreams.

He walks down the stairs, pushes open the door to the lobby, lights a cigarette, and smokes, taking long drags. The puffs of white smoke mingle with the damp fog that fills the air around him. He can hear birds chattering in the forest as the sun sets.

He's about to leave, because he must, but a hand lands on his shoulder.

"Stay a little longer," says Alex.